# The Whole *of the* Heart

GILIANNE HEITMAN

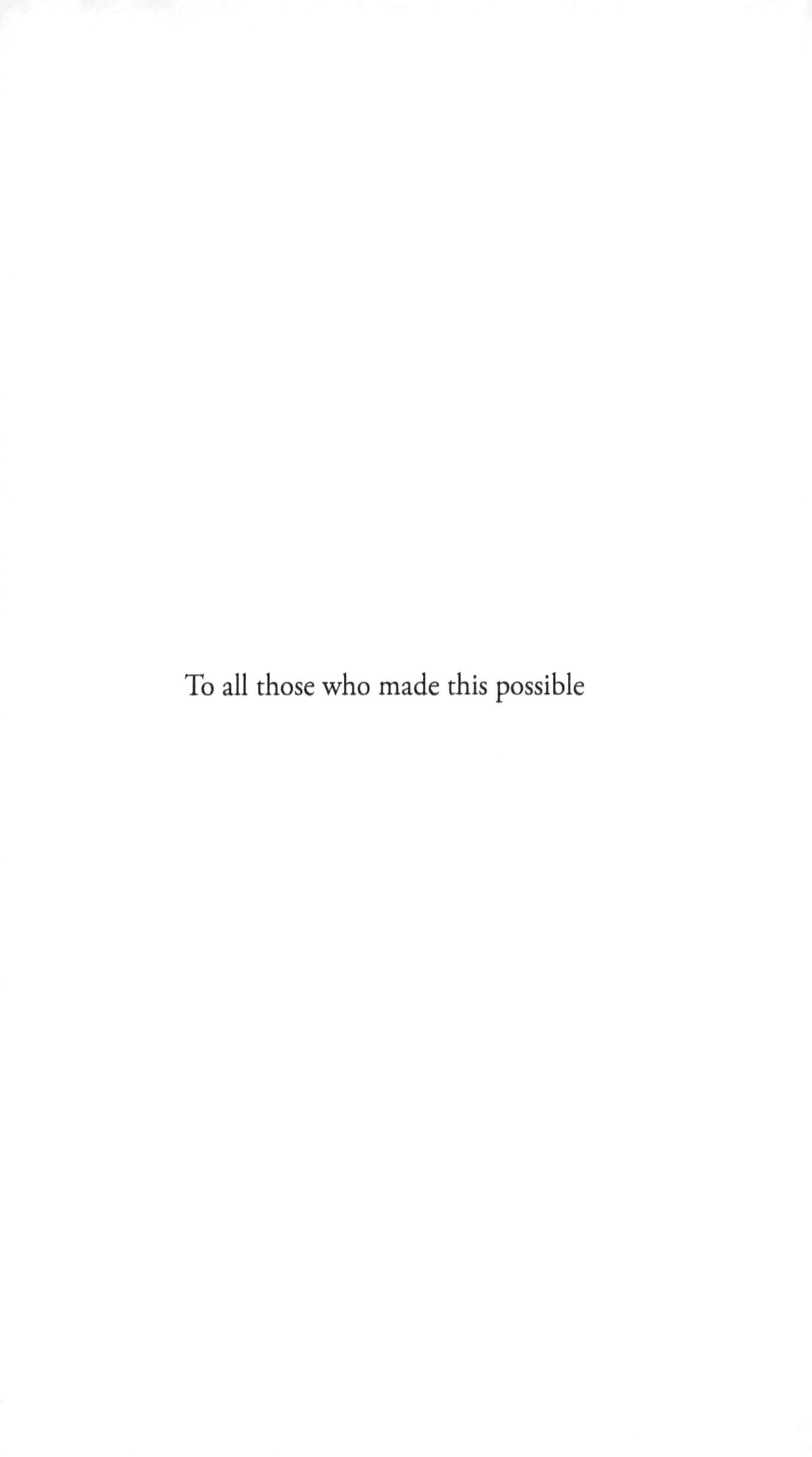

To all those who made this possible

# Chapter One

## 21 February 1893

The house whines of Father's absence. The walls shift from the simple weight of the wind without the support of the head to hold them up. Doors latch in their frame before letting go. Floorboards upstairs creak, mocking me of my loneliness tonight. Air howls as it tunnels down the two hallways branching out from the top of the stairs, inflating each room with enough to fill them entirely.

Father should be home by now.

"It's time for him to be back," the house whispers slyly between groans and heaves. "It's time to come home."

As I sit, the step under me shrieks in solidarity with the house, staring at the entryway for Father. Scotland Yard shouldn't keep him at this hour. Once he leaves in the morning, I am alone until he returns, with nothing but my thoughts and surroundings to keep me busy. There's no doubt he's been assigned an active case to solve. The nights Captain gives him a new file are the only nights he stays away from home so late. It's been a few weeks since he's brought one home, one worthy enough to risk it all to surprise me. He'd never leave me home so long for anything else; surely that must be it.

Moonlight floods the room, and the house breathes a sigh of relief as the front door opens and Father takes a step in.

"I'm so sorry, Annie," he laments, closing the door behind him. "The Chief wanted me to stay late tonight, but I tried to leave as soon as possible. Have you been waiting long, darling?"

"Oh," I say, running into his arms. "You're home now and that's all that's important."

"You must be starving! Let's go to the kitchen, and I can make dinner. It's about time you go to bed!" He laughs, and the warm glow of the house returns as the flames in the oil lanterns down the hallways burn brighter under his smile.

"What did you do at work today?" I ask, following him down the hallway.

Stone floors support the large wood table in the center of the room, and the fire-burning stove top rests on the other side, its red eye staring at the four legs. Metal pots and pans hang from the rack above the stove, and the shelves next to it beg to be used again to store more food than a solitary apple.

"Just the usual." He plops a blue folder on the table between us.

"Is that a new case?" The excitement swells from my chest and into my voice, but I can't help it.

"What do you think it is?" He chuckles softly again. "I trust you've seen enough of these to know."

My hand flies across the table, reaching to flip it open, desperate to solve another mystery.

"Ah." He yanks it back as I touch it, moving it just out of reach. "First, tell me what you did today."

"I found another rock in the garden!"

"Oh, really?" He raises his eyebrow, grabs a carrot, and rapid tapping of the knife on the table begins as he slices it. "What makes this one special enough to join your collection?"

"It is perfectly round! And smooth!"

He cannot contain himself as his hearty laugh echoes through the walls, bouncing off the stone floors. "Well, that certainly meets the criteria! Where do you find the room to keep all of these rocks?"

He tosses the carrots into a metal pot and reaches for the cabbage, just like I've seen him make this a hundred times, and I can recount each step perfectly, just as I remember every story he's told me from the bookshelves upstairs. Father worries I would burn the house down if I were to make it, though, so the two of us spend the evenings cooking and eating together. Tonight it is vegetable stew. Again.

"That is classified information!"

"I suppose this has nothing to do with the creaky floorboard in your room." He raises both eyebrows. "I hear you pry it out of your floor at night."

"Not anymore!" I scowl, defeated that my secret has been spoken into existence.

"Where are your shoes?" He looks up from the table, placing his hands on his hips. "They'd better be outside on the porch, little miss. You know the floors inside should stay clean from the mud!"

"Yes, I left them on the porch! How could Scotland Yard's best detective miss such a clue?"

"I've been bested by my own child! At twelve years old, no less! Ah, well, there's no choice but to relinquish that title now! Whoever will take my place?" The leaves slosh in the broth in the pan as Father throws it in. "I guess the only worthy opponent is the one who can solve this case!" He slides the folder back across the table toward me. Vegetable scraps fly on the floor as I fling the file open. "A woman is missing. She is a wife and a mother who escaped from Bethlem Royal Hospital—"

"She escaped from an asylum?" I interrupt, too impatient for Father to waste time with irrelevant information. "How did she do it?"

"That's what we are trying to find out. The nurses noticed she was gone when they did their rounds to check on her in the morning. Nothing was out of place. She just vanished." A cloud of dust comes between us as he wipes the table clean before the dull thud of the knife passing through the potatoes begins. "We spoke to her family and checked her house, but she was not there."

"Of course, she wouldn't go there! She's not stupid," I say, dumbfounded that he would make such a foolish statement.

"She was in the asylum, darling. You never know how people like her are or what they're thinking," he whispers, hoping not to offend any ghosts overhearing our conversation.

"I know she would want to stay away from her family and home!"

"But her home is familiar! It could very well be all she knows. She doesn't know any better."

"She's still a person. Capable of living, breathing, and thinking, just as you and I." I gesture to the both of us. "Besides, she was wrongfully sent there."

"Oh, really?" he hoots. "What is your proof to support this bold statement?"

I point to her husband's information on the second line of her file. "This shows that she is his third wife within a short period. I'm sure the husband has another woman waiting, ready to be next. If you read her papers, she has no history. There is no proof of violence to herself or others." I flip through the pages, showing a list with nothing of note that could be used against this woman. "She is wise enough to escape and stay hidden. I suspect you should look into her husband for sending her away on false pretenses." I close the file and push it back across the table.

Father's eyes dart down to the stack in front of him, and then at me. Back and forth his eyes go, trying to put the two pieces of the puzzle together. "No! That cannot be right," he breathes. "Surely…"

Stew splatters as I throw potato chunks into the pot one by one, watching them swirl with the other vegetables while waiting for Father to process this information.

He raises his hands to his head and lifts them, taking the invisible crown off. "I believe this belongs to you, Annie. You solved the case, so surely you are the only one worthy of such an esteemed title." He moves his hands over my hair and places them on the top. "I now declare you Scotland Yard's finest detective!"

"Thank you." I curtsey. "I'll only carry this burden for a short while. We can work for Scotland Yard together when I'm older and split the responsibilities!"

"Oh, darling." His eyes droop as he looks at me. "I do not think that will happen. You are the best part of my life. If anything happened to you…" He trails off. "Why, it'd be too much to bear. The others at Scotland Yard will not be welcoming. You'll have more to fear within those walls than from the criminals on the streets. They'll do whatever it takes to get ahead at your expense, and I could do nothing to change it! I think you'd be better suited for marriage, my dear. That's the only life guaranteeing your happiness and safety, especially once I'm gone."

"Is this really what you want for me?" I blurt, shoving the file up to his face. "Do you think this woman felt happy or safe while her husband signed her life away as she watched, powerless to do anything?"

"Of course not! But—" Rapid knocks on the front door stop him from going further. "I'll be right back. Stay here, and we'll talk about this when I return. Keep stirring the soup so it does not burn!"

He disappears from view, roaming down the hallway until the squeal of the door rattles throughout the house. Indistinct and stressed words are exchanged between Father and our guest, but I am too far out of range to piece them together.

"Annie." Father runs back into the room. His ragged breath is barely enough to keep him standing. "I must leave straight away!"

"Again?"

"I am sorry, but the Chief needs my help to settle an urgent matter that has just risen a couple streets down. I'll be back soon, but dinner should be finished now." He walks over to the fire and moves the pot off for me. "Eat and go to bed, darling!"

"But we always eat dinner together…"

"Hudson and community need me tonight. Please try to understand. It's just a few hours, and then we can go back to normal tomorrow." Father straightens his back and salutes. "Constable Annie Yoder!"

"Are you saying—"

"I'm saying, as the times change, there may be more room for me to wiggle you into Scotland Yard when you're older."

"Promise?"

"I promise to try everything I can. But Hudson is waiting for me outside, and I must leave now. We'll talk tomorrow, Annie. I love you." He pops his head back through the door frame. "Keep the windows shut while I'm gone. I think there is a nasty storm coming." And just like that, he is gone.

# CHAPTER TWO

## 22 February 1893

The clock strikes two-twenty-two in the morning, just as it did the day before and every day prior. The deep chimes from the hallway are not enough to wake me most nights, but tonight it is all I can hear. The steady *tick, tick, tick,* from this broken clock rattles between the furniture in the library, mixed with the last words Father told me a few short hours ago. *Tick.*

*Tick.* The windows are closed and will remain so until the fierce wind settles and the rumble from the clouds subsides. *Tick.* The patter of the raindrops on the glass begins, masking the incessant ticking of the clock.

A gentle rap echoes through the chamber as the stars rattle in their glass frames, quiet as a butterfly's wings beating against the panes. It's just the bony branches of the tree rattling the windows, nothing more.

The flames in the fireplace thunder, illuminating every nook and cranny of this room, unearthing every secret. Its roar bellows through the room's four corners, scaring away unwanted intruders. The shadows slither down the walls and crawl back to the depths from which they came. Light flickers from the lanterns, warding the darkness from returning to the hidden spots it previously resided in.

Here I lie in the solitude of my mind and the worlds inside. Here I am transported once the library's contents are opened. I let my thoughts run free in the sanctuary of this room and allow them to seep between the pages, hoping to find a place to rest for a bit.

A room full of various worlds and people, but the blue back of Father's chair is the only thing to offer me company. An empty seat in a library brimming with life sits across from my own chair and stares at me, reminding me of my solitary curse tonight.

The floorboards outside the door groan as old bones do in a weary body. The rest of the beams of the house grumble in the same song of tiredness.

As he said, it would just take a little while to sort out his work.

Each raindrop grows louder and more forceful until fists begin banging on the windows and walls, rattling the house's frame.

Father should be home now. It's been many hours. Should I be concerned?

*Thud, thud, thud.* Pounding on the door is almost indecipherable from the storm raging on outside, but this could be Father. It has to be.

Plain green wallpaper whirls past me in the hallways as I race to the door and turn the handle. Before I can open the door, it is pushed in, and another child steps in. The confidence he exerts commands the room. He is the only thing I can focus on until his bright, droopy scarlet blazer burns my eyes. His face is sunken in, and his clothes hang from his body. Can he not afford new ones that fit him better?

"What are you doing?" I exclaim. "You cannot just barge into my house!"

"I do apologize, miss," he says coyly. "I am here on behalf of your father. If there is an issue, you can discuss it with him." His voice matches the authority his knock exhibited as he paints his face with a smirk.

"No, it is no problem," I breathe out, not wanting to tell him I am alone behind these doors. "I only meant to ask who you are."

"My name is Yvon Theodore Ambrose." He extends his hand toward me. "But others call me Teddy."

My breathing begins to grow faster, and my hand trembles as I hold it out for him to shake. "And I am—"

"I know who you are, Ann." He rolls his eyes as if my response annoys him. "How else do you think I got here? To the esteemed Yoder house!"

Butterflies thump their wings furiously against my stomach as my heart skips a beat. I stick my head out the front door and look down the street, but no one is lurking. How does the boy know me? How did he find me?

"Your father…" he begins slowly.

"What about him?" I snap.

"He responded to a call a few streets down…"

"I'm well aware," I say, holding my head high, knowing my father is a brave man willing to help others. After all, he is one of Scotland Yard's only constables with an ounce of human decency and morals.

"I'm afraid… he won't be returning."

"No," I say. This word is the only one I can force out. It's not possible. "The Chief would've sent someone else, a constable, not a child."

"A child?" He gasps. "I'll have you know we appear to be the same age."

"I appreciate your concern," I say, pushing him closer to the threshold again. "But I assure you my father is fine. Go back to your family. I'm sure they're worried about you."

"You needn't concern yourself with my family, miss. My nearest relative is a boat ride away." He lets out a dry laugh before continuing. "You are a fool to refuse help from me. I answered the call and now offer my services to you. You need me, Ann."

"I do not need anyone, and I certainly do not need you," I rebut. "You are the fool if you truly believe I am willing to enlist the help of a stranger. I would like you to leave, please."

He leans in close to me until I can smell a faint whiff of rot and ruin on him. He whispers, "When can we meet again?"

His eyebrow arches as he awaits the answer to this question. I am taken aback by the directness of his comment.

A small smile begins to form at the corners of his mouth. It's contagious. The corners of my own mouth turn up, despite my wishes. His iron grip wraps around my upper arm, pushing me further into the house. The voice in my head screams. Alarms sound in my head, and my body goes numb. What is happening? What is he doing? The thoughts become frantic as he slams the door. He releases me, and I am liberated from his grasp. I lunge toward the door, but he keeps his hand on the knob.

"The constables are walking up the street now! If they see the two of us alone..." He trails off.

My reputation would be ruined. Father would be destroyed.

"Hide!" I yell before he can continue any further. He scurries up the stairs and out of sight in the direction of the library. The quick brush of his red blazer against the darkness of the hallways appears to be a lamp beckoning others to follow him down the twisted veins of the house.

The soft, sharp knocks match the painful stabs in my heart from the quickening of my heartbeat. I yank the door open. "Father?" I ask.

Instead of his friendly, familiar face, I am slapped with the stale smell of cigars.

"No, child, it is not your father," a booming voice replies. He places his hand on my shoulder before continuing. "I'm afraid your father won't be returning." His words are slow, driving the knife of despair further into me. "Tonight, your father died heroically, saving others."

"No," I whisper. There is no point in denying it now. "No!"

"I am very sorry, child," he continues, each pat on the top of my head is bone-shattering. "But know you will be looked after. If you can find a family member to take you in for a short while, I will be able to offer you help in a few years' time. I owe it to your father. I owe him a great debt, indeed, and he would want me to make sure his pride and joy is taken care of," he mumbles, smiling softly. "A service will be held later in the week as a tribute to one of Scotland Yard's finest! I will handle the planning of the funeral myself. I would also like to escort you there to say your goodbyes."

Each word fades into the night, swirling up into the sky like wisps of smoke.

"Is there anyone you know of who can help? Anyone you can write to?"

I nod my head, knowing there is not a soul who can, but I want to rid the house of this person. The hinges creak as I begin to close the door.

"Remember, ask for George Hudson should you find yourself needing help!" He manages to huff out before the door closes in his face.

"As I said earlier," a voice squeaks over the railing of the stairs.

"Please…" I heave. "Leave me alone!" I yell.

He raises his hands defensively, shaking his head as if shaking away my request. "All right, all right. I will leave you alone! But I will remain here with you to help you until someone else can. You may not realize it now, but you will see what I can do."

Are there any other choices? Anyone else to turn to? I know the answer as well as he does. He smirks as he steps away and disappears further into the house, his dark crimson blazer fading from view.

I roam the hallways with a knife through the heart. Hours go by, and shadows creep as there is no more laughter or smiles to reflect off the surfaces inside. I watch as the glow of my childhood fizzles as all candles do eventually, but I feel like mine was only just lit.

# Chapter Three

## 26 February 1893

The vibrancy of the green damask wallpaper and red carpet in the corridors diminishes beneath the trail of Teddy's muddy footprints. This sludge now infects every room of the house. Windows and mirrors cloud as there is nothing worth showing anymore. No part of my home is safe from being ravaged by this mess.

"Teddy!" I grumble as I follow the thick layer of cemented mud to the library. "This room is filthy! There is no one else but us to clean this up!" His footprints trail a line of books along the walls inside.

"Then I suppose you should stay and take care of it," he banters, laughing from his chair.

"You know I can't do that, not now."

"Are you sure you want to go to that today?" He glances up from his book.

"To my father's funeral?" I snap. "Yes, I'm sure I want to go!"

"But will you know anyone? Will they even know you? Have you ever met any of his fellow constables?"

The rapid fire of his questions barely gives me time to think before responding.

"He left me all alone with nothing and no one! Of course I won't know anyone there!" I say, exasperated. "All I know is that George should be here soon, so you," I point assertively at him, "should keep out of sight."

"But what am I supposed to do all evening?" he whines.

"Clean up your mess! But you need to stay inside. Keep out of the garden!"

"But—"

"You are free to leave whenever you'd like if you don't like the rules!"

"You know I have no one else to live with! We are the same in that way," he notes, putting his book on the floor as he sits up. "What other loveable twelve-year-old would you find to help you build your rock collection?"

Ah, the collection that remains untouched under my room's floorboards. Father was never happy to find those pesky presents left over the floors. Yet, this practice resumed when Teddy moved in, albeit with a new hiding place.

"Someone who can take care of their own mess!" I joke.

I groan as my toe strikes the hard-shell suitcase sticking out too far by the door. My initials gleam in the gold lettering on the side of my already packed belongings. If a long-lost relative, or god-willing, agent from the orphanage surfaces, I suppose I should be ready to leave at the drop of a hat.

His grumbles echo through the house, but I begin walking to the door before he begins his protests. With each step toward the door, the dull knock strikes my ribcage as I dread facing the other side.

"Hello, Annie!" George chirps, offering the first smile this house has seen for several days.

"It's just Ann now."

"Oh. I do apologize—"

"The only person who called me that is dead."

Without a word, he opens the yellow metal door. I take his hand as I step in, leaving the both of us to stew in the awkwardness of unfamiliarity. He closes the door behind him, and the horses begin pulling the carriage with two strikes of his cane.

The blue leather seat stares back at me, asking me what I should say to ease the tension.

"Again, I am sorry for your loss," George says, taking the first stab at this unknown creature between us.

"Thank you."

"I wanted to ensure intimacy today, so I assure you there will be a limited number of people. I do not want to overwhelm you, child." He waits a moment before continuing, perhaps waiting for a response. "I never heard back from your family. Is someone coming to look after you?"

My nod satisfies him, and although this is not the truth, it is not a complete lie. I suppose he is not related to me, but Teddy is offering some help.

"What did he do?" I ask, shattering the ice.

"I'm sorry?"

"How did my father die?"

He is astonished by my question and can barely string together enough words to make a coherent sentence.

"I am not sure that is appropriate for such a young girl!" He gasps.

"He is my father, and I have a right to know!"

"I suppose you are right," he concedes with a solemn head shake. "There was a skirmish involving an unsettled dispute with a factory owner and a group of workers. I was called down to help settle it, and I stopped and got your father on the way, as I'm sure you are aware by now. When we arrived, the situation escalated far faster than we anticipated. Someone brought a gun and started shooting. I was stuck in the crossfire. But your father pushed me out of the way and took a bullet that should've been for me."

Silence. Nothing distracts from the gushing wound filling the carriage and drowning us in the blood of remorse or from the single tear on our faces as the horses slow in front of Scotland Yard.

"Now is as good a time as any to go inside. Your father can't wait for us forever." He chuckles lightly. He opens the door, steps out, and offers his hand for me to step down.

I have seen it many times with my father during my adventures in the city. The fortified exterior of the station lies before me. The unpenetrated brick wall exudes the force necessary to intimidate those walking by. The spaced white horizontal lines offer temporary relief from the aggression of the red surrounding it, and the abundance of windows resting across the entirety of the exterior allows those inside to overlook the people down below with their callous, judging eyes.

I take one step forward, followed by another, and another, until I reach the front door. George stands at the entrance, waiting for me to cross the threshold.

From the doorway, the stuffy air of grief suffocates me. Here I stand on the edge between what is alive and dying. Is it too late to turn back? Maybe Teddy was right.

Before I can spin around, the Chief nudges me into the room. And so I fall into the arms of Death, and he catches me like a familiar friend.

There's a wooden coffin on a platform directly ahead, and that is all I focus on. Everything else in the room fades to the background because it is irrelevant. The floorboards and rows of desks do not mean anything when they offer nothing but distance between my father and me.

"How did you know Arthur?" a lady next to me whispers.

"He was my father," I respond, turning to face the stranger.

"Oh," she utters softly. "Oh!" she says again as if remembering something important. "You must be little Annie!"

"It's just Ann," I correct her.

"Your father often spoke of you. You've grown up so much since the last time I saw you! It's been—"

"Who are you?" I ask, uninterested in entertaining a stranger.

"I do apologize," she replies, holding her hand out for me to shake. "I am Alexandra Yeats."

Yeats?! Everyone in the city knows of the family. Whispers of the legitimacy of their wealth crawl down every street. The lampposts tell of the haste in which their marriage was founded. The carriages reveal the sordid company and pastimes Alexandra kept. The cobblestones query where the money to live in such a beautiful house comes from. The people passing by their permanently locked gates question what goes on within those four walls.

"Ah, Mrs. Yeats!" George interrupts our conversation before I can ask her any more questions. "I'm glad you could come. I haven't heard anyone whispering of stolen horses yet or I would've known you were here! I know Arthur would've been happy to see you here. He often told stories of the shenanigans you two got into."

"It's been many years since we've done anything of the sort." She chuckles.

"Will your children be joining us?"

"They never knew him. That chapter of my life started when the one with Arthur closed. It's been proven time and time again that this city is not safe. I suspect the gates will remain locked for a while longer in light of this tragedy. The thought of losing anyone else in my life…" She trails off. "Well, it's a thought I cannot bear to entertain."

"My father never spoke of your relationship with him," I interrupt, trying to change the subject.

"Well, I cannot say that I'm surprised. It feels like a lifetime ago. The legality of some of our extravaganzas may be questionable, but memorable none-theless." A faint smile turns up at the corner of her mouth.

"What did you do?" I ask, elated at the thought of hearing yet another one of my father's legendary stories.

"These are tales for another time, dear. Now it is time to say goodbye to your father."

"But I am not ready," I say, wiping away the tear on my cheek before she comments.

"You will never be ready for such a thing, Ann, but you must do it to move on." She takes my hand before continuing, "The world will give you many rotten apples, but it is necessary for you to learn to accept them with grace."

"But I don't want to accept them. Why should I?"

"I suppose nothing is forcing you to, but there is nothing that can be done to change what has already happened. Ladies such as us are not given much choice in the matter. A rotten apple is offered to you now. You can throw it to the ground or hold it in your hand, but the apple is still there."

She gently drops my hand and walks up to the coffin, placing her hand on the top.

What do I do with this apple? Do I accept it? Do I throw it?

I take one step forward, and another, following in the same footsteps as Mrs. Yeats.

# Chapter Four

## March 1, 1893

"Annie, we are all out of apples," Teddy's voice carries from the kitchen.

"Well, what do you expect me to do about that?" I quip jokingly.

"We have no more of anything, really."

"Already? The cabinets were full just last week!" All his help evidently is not free. If he continues, the rest of Father's saved money will fly out the window from under the floorboards by the end of the year! "We cannot keep—"

"Going out!" he finishes. "I agree. But we need to eat! I can bring us apples and food."

He is right, I suppose. "Oh, all right." I grin as the stresses absolve into the air between us. "Just a quick trip into the city markets. Besides, no one has seen us through the drawn curtains and closed door. We should be in the clear."

"Do not be so naive, Annie! People could still know. They could've still seen the shadows or heard the voices."

"I hardly believe—"

"Need I remind you," he interrupts, "you are the one who stands to lose everything if we are not careful. You are the one who will be cast to the streets, ruined and destitute. We are unmarried and living together. If we cannot hide this…" He trails off, leaving the rest up to my wild imagination.

The damage is done from whatever has happened in the past. Asking Teddy to leave now would only result in me staying under this crumbling roof on my own. Besides, if I kicked Teddy out, there would be nowhere else for him to go. It's not a possibility. I'm not sure I even want him to go, though, because who am I without him here? Behind these heavy, embroidered curtains is nothing but stories whispered between the two of us or the whiny floorboards under our feet as we explore the rooms. No one else beyond the front door, let alone the iron gates, will know of the days passing us within these four walls and will never know of the lives we've really lived.

"We'll just need to be extra cautious while we go into the city then, I suppose. If we go now, we should catch the shop owners before they close," he instructs, holding his hand out for me.

"Is it wise for us to go together?" I start. "Maybe we would lower our risk of getting caught if we went separately…"

"Don't be ridiculous." He chuckles. "If you go alone, without a chaperone, it would draw just as much attention. And you've made it abundantly clear that you do not trust me to go on my own." He scowls.

"We have to be careful of how much we spend," I start. "Once Father's money is gone, there is nothing else. And you don't seem like you are cautious enough."

He continues scowling. "I suppose. So I guess we are going together then?"

"It would appear so," I respond. "We must leave now if we wish to buy anything."

"Perhaps you should wear a bonnet…"

"A bonnet?" I exclaim. "Those have not been the fashion in decades!"

"One could prevent people from recognizing your face. Surely you must have one here."

"Don't you think I will draw more attention by wearing it?"

"I think that is a risk we should take. If people stare, you can look down, and they won't be able to see anything to identify you."

"I can possibly wrangle an old one from my dresser that's been there for ages. Wait here, and I'll be right back!"

I run up the stairs and rummage through my drawers. Black silk hiding in the shadows from the back corner greets my fingers, and I yank it out. The cool blade of metal stings the tips of my fingers as I yank my hand out. No sound comes from the floorboards when the bonnet hits the ground but a stifled gasp escapes from my mouth. One by one, handkerchiefs and gloves fall around the bonnet as the drawer is stripped of its covers until there is nothing but a silver knife inside. Metal vines curve up the handle, reaching for the blade to cut them free.

Where did this come from? Surely I would remember putting this in my drawer, right?

"Annie, are you coming?" Teddy calls up the stairs.

I shove the drawer into the dresser and yank the bonnet on my head, trying to cram all my hair into the back and secure it by tightly tying the ribbon under my chin.

I race back to the top of the staircase and yell, "I'm ready!" before thudding down. Teddy stands by the front door, holding it open for me.

The sun's rays stab my eyes as I take one step across the threshold. This is the first time I have been outside since my father's funeral. This is the first source of natural light I have seen in ages. Evidently, the oil lanterns pale in comparison to the sun's rays.

The two of us walk through the yard and the iron gates of the property, closing them firmly behind us. The soft clamor and hubbub rise above the quickly diminishing sunlight of the setting sun over the bustling city. Nothing more than scattered words and sounds funnel through the bonnet and into my ears. Teddy walks next to me, each stride matching mine; our feet hit the path at the same time. Too afraid to look the world in the eye, all I can see is our footsteps falling in sync.

Air is sucked from my lungs, and the thick cloth of smoke is shoved down my throat in its place. As the empire of factories rose higher than the historic buildings and defeated them with their industrialized weapons, little of the old ways of nature were preserved.

"Do you know where you're going?" I ask.

"Of course!" He laughs. "You're not the only one who has been to this city. We can cross through this alley, and the storefront should be not too far up the street."

He nudges me into the shadows of this unknown path. I glance at him to make sure that he knows what he is doing before taking my foot off the cobblestone. He nods and takes one step behind me, gently nudging my shoulder.

I tell my racing heart that we are almost there, but the butterflies flutter relentlessly.

"Please!" a voice rasps, booming as it echoes between the buildings. "Help an old lady!"

Sprawled on the ground, I see a haggard woman with nothing but the building wall to support her back. Her tattered clothes offer scant protection from the bare teeth of the wind and rocks, doing nothing to stop the bleeding from the scrapes across her body. The streaks of gray in her brown hair reflect the sun.

"Do you have any family? A husband? Children? Someone who can help you?" I ask, stooping down to look her in the eyes.

My skirts are not thick enough to shield my knees from being jabbed by the jagged stones sticking up from the road. Her shoulder jerks from the palm of my hand when I touch her.

"Please! Is there anyone you can ask for help?"

She spits on the street, next to my boot. "The only person who could've done any good left long ago. 'Course, that was the best thing he did!"

"Would your husband consider—"

"Husband? Ha!" Her green eyes pierce me as she finally looks up. "I have no husband, dearie. Never have, and never will."

Oh. Surely she must have someone. "Is there a family member we can ask?"

"No," she moans, her voice quivering. "Not anymore, that is. My children, they're gone."

Gone? When will they be back? Why would they abandon their own mother in this state?

"B-but, they said I murdered them! It wasn't me!" She grabs my arm, clawing at my skin as she pleads her case. "Please believe me! I didn't kill my children! They were starving!"

"I do! I believe you!" I cry.

"They were dying. The poison would've helped them anyway," she rasps, heaving between words. Reaching up to grab my hand robbed her of the last ounce of energy.

"I understand, there—"

"Stop!" Teddy hisses, yanking me away from the woman. "Who are you talking to?"

"She needs help!"

"Who?"

"The woman!" I exclaim, pointing down to her. "She needs help! We have to do something!"

"There's no one there, Annie. We need to leave before you make a scene!'

"No! We need to help her. She has no one else who can save her."

"It sounds like she did this to herself then, if there is no one to save her! If she has no husband, no family, and no money, nothing can save her."

Nothing. If the roles were reversed, what would happen? If someone notices me on these streets, will this be me? Nothing more than a woman begging for her life, pleading for mercy at the expense of her sanity.

"No," I say, defeated. "She's right there!"

"I can assure you, there is nothing here but the two of us."

"I need to leave," I squeak.

"What? What about the food? What do—"

"Here." I yank my coin purse from my waist and shove it into his hands. "Use this. Buy as many apples as you want and whatever else you think we need. I cannot stay here. If I am recognized…"

"What has gotten into you?" he cries.

"I have to go. I can't risk it! Do not cross the gates until it is dark and no one can see you!"

Smoke swirls around me, keeping me hidden from other pedestrians as I run back to my house. Looking over my shoulders, no one is behind me, so I continue. Uneven cobblestones poke my feet through the thin soles of my shoes, but not even a little blood can stop me before I get home.

The metal spikes on top of each bar from my gate stab the smoke cloth, and at the sight of their tips, I am finally home! The latch turns as I unlock it, and I turn the key once more as soon as I step to the other side of it. Did I lock it? I yank on the bars, but it does not budge. Good. I scurry up the path and through the door before anyone can see me.

The door swings inward, and the remaining sunlight illuminates the tracks on the red rug.

"Teddy!" I grumble to myself. "Stop trailing mud in the house!" But I know I am the only person who is listening. How can he trail so much into the house all the time? Where does it all come from? There are no exposed patches in the yard.

Dust and dirt cling to my palms as I crawl through the house, inspecting every nook and cranny for any visibility from the streets. Every curtain receives an extra tug, every window latch is tightened, and every door is securely locked for safe measure.

I reach the door to my room and push it in from the bottom, determined to get inside and put the knife back in the kitchen where it belongs. I pick up the clothes littering the floor as I inch over them on the way to the dresser. Once the curtain is firmly pulled, I race over to the drawer and yank it open. The empty bottom stares back at me.

Where did it go? Who took it out? Did someone else break into my room while Teddy and I were out?

I shove the handkerchiefs and gloves back inside, slamming the drawer shut. I take one step back, and continue taking one step at a time, afraid to turn my back on this monstrosity of a mystery.

Teddy is the only one coming back through these doors. Nothing outside of the iron gates can justify the risk of leaving this house again. My foot will not touch the grass, and my skin will never bask in the warmth of the sun's rays again. Teddy can sneak out and buy our food under the cloak of the night sky from now on. He has remained undetected in the city thus far and can continue.

# Chapter Five

## 22 February 1896

"Are you okay?" Teddy's voice greets me in the hallway outside the library. I stand up from my chair and poke my head from the door.

"I can't sleep," is all I can say.

"It is a special day, I suppose," he whispers. "An odd anniversary."

"I keep thinking of what will happen now.... after so little has changed. What am I supposed to do?"

"There is no limit, Annie." He offers his hand out to me, as he did two years ago. "Would you care to dance in the yard beneath the moonlight? It's quite the magnificent ballroom." He chortles, pulling me into his iron grip.

"What if people can see us outside?" I ask, panicked at the thought of being spotted.

"No one will," he groans.

One firm head shake is enough to convince him I will not cross through the front door.

He sighs. "Will the hallway suffice? The curtains have been drawn for ages. No one will know."

I agree.

Indulging in this dance, we waltz through the corridor beneath the flickering flames of the lamps mounted on the walls. With each step back, there are two steps forward as we inch to the back of the house, closer and closer to the shadows.

"What is your plan, Ann?" he queries, chuckling at his unintended rhyme.

"We have lived here, undiscovered for years without anyone noticing. I think we can continue for a little longer."

"But what about after that?"

"I don't know. I think I can worry about that later—"

"When you have been kicked to the street?" he interrupts. "When it's too late to do anything?"

He's right. "I can take the Chief up on his offer and see—"

"But it isn't clearly defined. He could give nothing, or he could've changed his mind."

"What about asking the Yeats? I met Alexandra at my father's funeral, and she seemed—"

"You cannot turn to a stranger for help! Don't you have any pride?!"

"Why must we stay in London?"

"Where else will we go? Where will we find the money to make it there? And once we get there, how will two children find enough to live off?"

Once again, he's right. One step back and two steps forward beneath the fire blazing inside the glass covers of the lanterns. The thin fingers of smoke float down the hallway and pour down the stairs.

"When we first met, you mentioned you have a family—"

"That is not a possibility, Annie," he rebukes. "We are not married, and you are not ready for the intense journey to get there."

"But Teddy! This could be my only way out! What other solutions—" I cry.

"Trust me," he says between his teeth. "It is not an option yet."

"Do you smell that?" I ask, changing the conversation.

"Smell what?" Two steps forward.

"The smoke." One step back.

"It's just from the lamps." Two steps forward.

"Are you sure?" One step back. "There's too much."

"I'm sure it's nothing," he dismisses, leading me one more step back.

And we dance beneath the flames, guiding us further into this convoluted maze of smoke and malaise, with the only certainty being each other. Two steps forward.

"Something's not right," I say, coming to a jarring stop.

"I told you, everything is fine!" He pushes me one more step back.

Windows rattle in their frames as a beam from the house below crashes down on top of itself.

"The house is on fire!" I yell.

"Are you sure?" he argues.

"The house is collapsing! We have to put it out!"

"And how do you plan on doing that? We cannot control the fire on our own if the damage is already destroying the body. We need to leave!"

"No! Where will I go?"

"I am not sure, but if we do not do something, we will die here!" he cries.

"We have to talk to Hudson."

"No, I said that's a bad idea," he chides, shaking his head.

"There's no other choice, Teddy. I want to grab—"

"We have no time! We have to leave now!" He grabs my hand, yanking me down the stairs and through the front door as the clock chimes behind us.

"But where are you going to go?" I gasp as we sprint into the street just outside of the gates.

"I'll manage to find somewhere to stay, but the city cannot find you in that house alone! You will be taken away!"

We run through the streets hand-in-hand, leaving my home to fend for itself amidst the flames. I abandon this chapter of my life as a person fleeing their family does in pursuit of a new life.

"Do you know where you are going?" I ask.

"Would I ever guide you in the wrong direction?" He gasps, feigning offense.

"Oh, I suppose not." I laugh as we arrive in front of a set of green doors. Scotland Yard.

"You must do this part alone, Annie."

He tries to let go of my hand, but I tighten my grip.

"We can find somewhere we can both stay! We can—"

"You know," he says softly, "we cannot do anything together right now that will not lead us down perilous paths. Marriage is out of the question because—"

"Because I'm far too young to give up the little liberties I have left," I interrupt.

"We are indeed too young." He nods. "I'm sorry, but you know why I can't go with you inside."

"For now," I say, releasing his hand. "You are not rid of me quite yet! It will take more persuading than that." I laugh.

"I would never dream of losing you, Annie. You and I are in this together from now on."

I take two steps toward the gate, and he takes one step back.

"Meet me here tomorrow night, Teddy."

"I shall see you then. Be careful with what you do in there, or we both may be without a roof over our heads!"

He darts into the night, and I walk up the pathway, pushing the door open.

"Hello?" I ask. The word rattles between the empty space inside. "Is anyone here?"

It's been two years since I've seen the overwhelming, never-ending line of desks down the corridors to my left and right. Although, the vacant area in front of me is more welcoming to me today without the threat of my father's dead body a few paces away. Instead, nothing fills that spot, and I'm not sure there is anything that could ever fill it like that again.

"Hello, little one. Who are you?" a kind voice questions from the shadows.

He emerges from the corridor, stepping into the bleak light from the lanterns so we can see each other clearly. His eyes emit the same kindness as his voice, sharing the color of his blue uniform.

"I am here to speak to George Hudson," I say, unsure if I should give any more information to this stranger.

"The Chief? How do you know Hudson?" He guffaws.

"It's important, and I need to talk to him. He told me to ask him if I need help."

"And who should I say is making this late-night emergency call? A family member?" he challenges, walking toward the other constable in the hallway.

"No," I say, following him. "Tell him it's Ann Yoder."

"Yoder?" He stops mid-step. "You're Arthur's kid?"

"Yes."

"Oh," he whispers. "I am so sorry for your loss. I would have seen you at the funeral, but Hudson said it was a little affair."

"I understand, but this is quite important, and I must speak to George!"

He winces as my words strike him. "Of course." He reaches the other man in a blue uniform before saying, "I need you to go alert Hudson and tell him it's urgent."

"But it's the middle of the night!" the other man exclaims.

"Tell him I sent you, and that it's an emergency. He will understand!"

The man rushes out the door without looking back, wasting no time retrieving George to solve this crisis.

"I'm Samuel," he announces. "I don't know if your father ever mentioned me, but we worked together for quite a while."

"My father spoke very little of his colleagues. Unfortunately, I know little about who he knew outside our home."

"Well, as luck would have it, there are too many stories for me to keep to myself. I guess I will have to share them with you!"

"I would like that very much!" I exclaim, unable to hide my excitement at the prospect of reliving those glory days of youth, even if just for a moment between the golden glow of stolen memories.

"I suppose now is as good a time as any to start." He guides me to the nearest desk along the wall to the right of the door, gesturing for me to sit across from him. "Did he ever tell you about the time he and an old friend stole a horse?"

"No," I say eagerly, hanging on to every last word.

"Well, it all begins—"

"What is the meaning of this at such a late hour?" George huffs as he waddles through the door, half-dressed in his night garments. "Don't you know I must be back here in a few hours?"

"Sir, she just came—"

"Ah, Miss Yoder," he says, recognizing me instantly. "Are you safe and well? What do you need?" He dismisses the constable who summed him before continuing.

"I have nowhere to go. No clothes, possessions, or family to look after me, and my home is…"

"The fire!" he blurts out, remembering the commotion in the streets earlier. "Are you hurt, child?"

"No, but I need somewhere to stay while I figure out where to go next."

"What happened? How did it start?"

"I don't know." The tears well in my eyes as the enormity of the situation hits me with the weight of an oncoming train. "The house just started crumbling, and I…"

"Do not worry, Ann. The basement houses extra furniture not used in the other rooms in the building. We can fashion a bed of sorts, and I can ensure that meals are brought down for you every night." He grabs a lamp from the nearest desk and begins walking down the hallway, beckoning Samuel and me to follow. "Can you read?"

"Is there not an extra bed in your house?" I ask, not wanting to spend my days confined to a basement.

He shakes his head slowly. "There is not enough room for my own family in our home as it is, and we cannot fit another person with another child on the way. The best I can offer you is this room." We reach the end of the corridor, and he opens a door revealing a set of stairs leading down toward a dark pit. "But be advised, no one can know of your presence there, or it will be all our heads on the chopping block."

I turn to Samuel with pleading eyes. Surely one of my father's friends would take me in!

"My tenement door is always open for a Yoder to visit. Please understand that I am scraping by to provide for myself. If I offered to care for you, it would not be a life worth living."

I nod my head solemnly, understanding despite my wishes.

"Well, come on. I don't have all night to wait for you!" George huffs from the bottom of the stairs. "Can you read?" he asks again.

"Yes, I used to read many books from my library," I respond as I blindly stumble from one step to the next.

Once I reach Hudson, I look around the room and wish the darkness would swallow me whole. There is nothing here besides two desks in the back of the room, buried beneath mounds of wilted papers and files. This is where I'm expected to live?

"In this corner," George guides Samuel and me to the opposite side of the room behind the staircase, "is a platform that will be a perfect place for a bed! Until I can wrangle a mattress up, we can use some of these old documents." He throws scraps on the wooden slats and stands back to admire his handy work.

Hudson hands me an open folder from another pile nearby. "Can you understand this?"

I glaze over the file, pointing to the words I don't recognize.

He looks over my shoulder, nodding at each word. "Arsenic is a type of poison. In this case, a mother gave it to her children."

I repeat the word, trying to say it exactly as George said. "Are you sure the mother would do such a thing?" I ask as my mind flies back to the woman on the street.

"Yes, child! Anyone is capable of such heinous crimes if you're willing to open your eyes and pay attention."

He continues defining the other words I pointed to, giving the most bone-chilling list of terms known to man. "I don't understand. Why do I need to know these terms?"

He hobbles over to the desk and flops the folder down on top of it. "There has been a surge in crime over the years, and we can't keep up with all the cases and paperwork. There are far too many—"

"You want me to stay down here and work on these files?" I interrupt.

Samuel takes a step forward. "She is just a child. She should not have to spend her youth—"

"Child or not, she has no home or family!" George turns to me before continuing. "You can choose to leave and refuse this offer. Yet, you will find yourself in the same situation wherever you go. No one will open their doors to you in exchange for nothing. Here, I can promise you privacy, food, and a job that does not put your life at risk. There are no machines that will cut your fingers off down here, but in any other place you run to, there will be. The choice is yours."

The decision is made for me, I suppose. I can bet my life in a factory outside or gamble away my sanity remaining locked away.

"Where do I find the files? On your desk?" I ask.

"No!" he yells. "You must never go further than the stairs! If you are seen, if anyone but us three learns that you are living down here and working on these cases, you will be cast to the streets, and we will not have our jobs anymore! Do you understand?"

I nod.

"I will leave files here," he points to the desk he threw the folder on earlier, "before I go home each night and will come to collect them when I come in the morning. When I deliver the file, I will bring food with it. Do you agree to these terms?"

I nod again, knowing there are no words to express the doubts beginning to gnaw away at the few thoughts I managed to keep hidden in the folds of my mind.

"Good," he huffs. "I'll drop off the first cases for you tomorrow." He staggers up the stairs. "Samuel, get back upstairs!" he barks from the top. "And do not whisper a word of this to a single soul!"

Samuel nods, following in George's footsteps. He turns to me before disappearing and says in a hushed voice, "I'm not often here during the night, but when I am, I can sit at this desk," he gestures toward the one sitting across from the one with the folder, "and we can work on the paperwork together. Of course, only if you would like that," he offers with raised eyebrows.

"I would like that very much!"

He smiles, and before I know it, I am alone again, standing in a room with nothing but myself. Father was right, in his own way, I suppose. I could become a constable someday, thanks to him.

# CHAPTER SIX

## 11 February 1898

There is no need to open the blue file sitting on my desk and release the wailing horrors back into the air once again. The seeds of doubt planted in my mind last night from the first glance of this case are now beginning to sprout. I have spent the night memorizing every facet of this disappearance. A child was stolen from his bed in the middle of the night without a trace. Only a star-shaped birthmark could distinguish him from anyone wandering the streets. How am I supposed to find him while shackled to this desk underground? How can I find the kidnapper with nothing of use?

Maybe Teddy could help. We planned to meet tonight, after all. Would Hudson approve of an outsider helping me? In smuggling this information past this fortress, would I be breaching the trust of Scotland Yard?

Teddy and I will be the only ones aware of this, and the night sky will guard me. No one outside of the two of us will know. It will be a secret again, just as we kept our secrets behind the closed curtains of my old home.

I climb up the stairs with the file in hand, slow enough to ensure not one board warns the skeleton crew of my presence. I race through the door wishing more than anything that I still had my old bonnet. But alas, there is nothing more of that life, and picking through the ashes will offer no solace to heal my soul.

"Finally," a familiar voice fusses. "I was wondering if you had forgotten."

"I could never." I smile, looking up at Teddy.

"It's nice to see you outside again, conquering your fears of the world."

"Ah, well," I say. "Staying in that basement all day is maddening. Nothing can be scarier than the deep corners of the mind sometimes."

"We should probably move away from here before someone spots us." He gingerly grabs my arm, and the two of us walk further down the sidewalk.

"Where are we going?"

"I suppose where we always go." He nods ahead. "It's pretty late. There shouldn't be anyone at the park now."

I nod, and we continue down the path alone. For as long as I can remember, it has been just the two of us, and it looks like it will stay that way.

"How was work today?" I ask.

"I had a grand time, as always." He laughs hollowly.

Working at the factory has taken its toll on him over the years, but no one else would take him in.

His smile crumbled, and his jokes dulled with the shine of his red vest. He is too young for Scotland Yard, and there is nowhere for him to hide in the basement with me. Work from sunrise to sunset gives him a bed and food. He should count himself lucky to have all his fingers and clothes that still fit him. If anything, his buttons will burst from his clothes if he cannot find new ones soon. He is quite lucky indeed.

"What do you have?" He points to my file.

"A top-secret document." I jokingly pull it closer to my chest. "It is classified information, and I'm afraid you don't have the clearance for it!"

"Is that so?" He raises his eyebrow and yanks the folder from my hand.

"I'll have you know that is illegal!"

"I suppose you'll have to arrest me then." He holds his hands out, feigning being put in shackles.

"It's a case I found on my desk this week that I can't seem to figure out."

He flicks the case open and skims the contents. "This is quite the conundrum," he says.

"Which is why I need your help. I'm not sure I can solve this one."

"But you have to figure this out! Or you'll end up where I am! If you're not careful, Hudson will kick you to the street!"

"Don't you think I know this already?" I howl. "You know this is what I've always wanted to do! Have you not listened to the stories of my father's cases I've told you of? I cannot mess this up and ruin my chances of becoming a Constable. That is why I need you!"

I do not like asking for Teddy's input on work matters, as I like to prove that I am capable and deserving of such work. Yet sometimes, I find it hard not to turn to someone.

"Are there any witnesses or family?"

"All the information his parents gave is in the file. There is nothing more than his absence to indicate anything is wrong!"

"And you're positive he was kidnapped?"

"Why else would his family report him missing?" I quip.

Teddy looks ahead, lost in thought. "The stars are beautiful tonight."

"What about the case!" I ask in disbelief.

"I need to think about it a little more. It is quite tricky."

A rip in the fabric of smog gives the bright pinpricks a chance to shine and be noticed. Even if just for a moment and even if only by the only two people outside. That is all life is in the end, noticing the brief holes of light in the cloth, no matter how many or how far away they are. The faint glow of their light guides us through the streets, leading us to the park.

A cobblestone path circles around a grassy knoll and is lined with benches and lamp posts hidden behind a fortress of trees. But we seldom dare to sit together on that hill as the constellations above may not be the only ones passing their judgment on those they shine for.

"Look at the flowers, Teddy!" I gasp, pulling him over to the bush by the nearest bench.

"A flower for my flower," he jokes, plucking it from the branch.

"You shouldn't have!" I huff. "It will die now!"

"All living things are made to die, Annie. It's just a matter of when and how."

"But there was still so much life left for it to live! You've cut it short!"

"And how can you possibly know how much longer it would've lived? For all we know, it could've started wilting tomorrow."

"Oh, all right! I suppose you are not wrong."

"How many times must you learn this lesson before you realize I am always right?" He chortles. "I can still see the whites of your eyes!" He glowers as I playfully roll my eyes.

"What shall we do tonight?"

"I'm quite tired, actually," he admits. "Would you mind if we sat for a while?"

"I suppose we have spent enough time together to sit and tolerate each other's company in silence."

"Eh." His head bobs in a mock indifference.

And so the two of us sit down on the bench under the protection of the branches and darkness. We only have one another. Where I end, he begins, and where he ends, I begin.

I rest my head on his shoulder and close my eyes, and his head bumps the top of mine as he follows suit.

"Teddy?" I ask.

"Hm?"

"How much longer must we live like this?"

"Like what, darling?"

"Surely there is someone we can ask for help," I whisper. The grass soaks up each word. "Why do we need to continue to hide like this? Our lives shouldn't be this difficult."

"But there is nothing we can do for this right now. If we ask, we risk exposing everything. Why jeopardize how we've lived this whole time?"

"It's just not fair!"

"It is the way of the world, my dear."

Together we sit like this, without any more words exchanged between us. Nothing more is to be said that has not been uttered before, but we are comfortable. So be it if this is the way we must continue for the rest of our days. Teddy is right. This has been our way of living for years. Why change it now? After all these years we have handled all of the different obstacles thrown at us, we can handle a few more. Right?

The dull weight of a red object falls from the branches looming over our heads and onto my lap. It's an apple! I hold it in my palm, leaning in to take a bite. My teeth sink into mush and my head recoils from this foul fruit. I peer inside the apple from where I bit into it and lock eyes with maggots wriggling underneath the red skin.

Launching the apple from my hand, I reel from this horror. Spitting the wretchedness of this apple on the grass does nothing to erase the texture or glistening eyes from my mind.

"Is everything all right, darling?" Teddy asks, keeping his eyes closed.

I look up to the spot where the apple landed, but there is nothing there. Not a shred of mush, peel, core, or maggot remains. I scan every piece of the trail and grass from arm's length, but it does no good. Where did it go?

"Yes, everything is fine, Teddy," I say, shaking my head.

It was a bad dream. I must've been asleep.

Hours pass and the two of us remain together, soaking in the solitude of the night until day breaks. The sun's rays begin tickling the green blades growing from the soil with their bright new arms. An orange halo ascends east, chasing out the shadows and ghouls creeping around the park.

"We need to leave!" I yank Teddy's arm up from the bench. "We stayed here all night and have little time to run back to our jobs before they realize!"

"It's daylight already?" he cries, enraged at the thought of the night, our only time of freedom slipping away once again.

"No one can find us! Will we meet again tonight?" I ask, my voice swelling with hope.

"Of course, darling. Just as we have every night before." His hand slips from my grasp as each of us runs our separate ways for now.

My thoughts flood my mind, ramming to the sides of my skull and allowing me to think of little else. My eyes do not embrace the forcible welcome back to the shattering reality of the prison in front of me. I hurriedly pass through the necessary thresholds and doorways to enter. The wind combs through the stray hairs that tickle my face, and my petticoats dance along my legs as I race down the hallway, yet time has slowed, leaving me to wade through its thick, syrupy consistency, fighting just to keep both feet firmly planted on the ground.

I have to retreat to the shadows before the other constables accuse me of breaking onto the property. The sun is coming up. How could I be so foolish? How could I have not paid closer attention to the time? I risked everything, for what? To ask Teddy about an unsolvable case?

A slight breeze kisses my ankles as I pick up my skirts to run down the stairs, each one letting out a stifled scream underfoot. However, I ignore these cries of protest, for I fear my heart will burst if I wait one second more. I reach the base of the steps, exasperated and out of breath, but that does not stop the chasm from opening within my chest once I look ahead.

"Hello, old friend. You know Hudson would not approve of these late-night expeditions of yours." Samuel's face stares at me from behind a lantern. "There will come a day when I cannot cover for you."

"I know. I know. I'm sorry, but sometimes I need to see something outside this prison." I pause, looking to see if his gaze softens in understanding.

"You chose to work here, and you are free to go at any time," he scolds.

"That's not fair!" I bark. "You know why I had to leave my home! You know I had no other choice! I had no house, no future, and nowhere to go!"

He sits in silence, his eyes staring at the wall behind me.

"It is nice to hear something aside from the heavy cries of the prisoners upstairs for once," I say softly, attempting to smooth over the ripples from the tiff.

"Ann…" He gazes upon me, searching my face, and I can see him contemplating his following words. He chooses to continue. "Hudson wants to see you now. He has been waiting since he arrived." His head tilts in the direction upstairs. Yet, he is trying not to look into my eyes.

"I fear you have grown obsessive and careless about the new cases over the last few days. The whispers of the ghost of Scotland Yard have returned."

"I appreciate your concern, but I want to remind you to mind your business!" I spit out, unable to contain the fiery rage from spewing forth from me as a fireplace cannot control embers burning those sitting too close to the coals. "I ask you kindly to observe your boundaries and not overstep them."

"When was the last time you solved a case?" he pries. "Or filed any paperwork? Hm?"

"I am trying to solve the disappearance of the Acker child!"

"That's the only one this week! Your carelessness is now affecting Hudson and I! Your decision not to take this work seriously is now crossing my boundaries! Someone with more experience would be better equipped—"

"More experience?" The ringing in my ears grows louder as I find I am struggling to hide my disbelief and anger. "I have plenty of practice and more brains than half of these fools. Be honest and reveal the real reason for your fear. Tell me the excuse for your so-called concern."

So this is what my father warned me of. Samuel is no friend of his!

"I assume you're familiar with the case?" he challenges.

"I have every word of this file engraved on my brain. Can you say the same?"

"As a matter of fact, I can. It made its rounds upstairs before being passed to the basement," he huffs. "Someone with more experience would be able to see that there are no clues, no leads, no family to ask. Without any of that, this case cannot be solved! Nothing more can be done!"

"Just leave me alone!" I shout. Unable to control the blood boiling under the surface, I push Samuel away and scream at him to go.

"I hate to turn my back on your father like this, but it's about time you face the consequences of your actions." He shakes his head as he creeps up the stairs. "Hudson is still waiting for you."

I am alone as I stand in this room and the ghosts from the past creep up on me. I cannot help but be transported to these same feelings from several years ago, under a hazy glow, banished to the bottom floor upon my first day at Scotland Yard, yet I remain almost as alone. However, now there will not be any stories of my father or chuckles traded between Samuel and I. This room will be forever haunted, endlessly cutting the wound of this broken relationship open again and again. When I lift my head and glance around the street, shattered glass and bricks fall on my shoulders as the world crashes around me.

# CHAPTER SEVEN

## 21 January 1901

Despite the lack of windows, there is enough light to read the headlines of the documents splayed over my desk. Although windows would not offer much help, the inky sky seeps in, spills on the desk, bleeds into the parchment, and makes the words indecipherable. Public indecency, thievery, kidnapping, murder, and the list of crimes are endless for me to solve during the witching hour.

My routine begins the same as every other night for the last six years. A soft whine from my battered mattress lets out as I sit up. The sagging bed droops, its edges brush the floor, and there is nothing to keep it supported because the thin slats have bent from the relentless burdens it had endured over the years. The sun goes down, and I am free to light the candles and search the case files for me to complete. Flickering flames guide me through the paper trail to find the culprits, each having left some clue for me to catch the guilty party. Find the file, find the damned. An endless cycle of monotony drags me from day to day like a doll being yanked by a child's arm, hoping this figment of their imagination will come true.

These four walls offer nothing; no memories, no privacy, no protection, and no sense of relief, but it is my only possession of this world, the only part of the world that proves my existence, and so I will cherish it. The deafening creak of each step from above screeches, howling to be released from this prison, but doomed to continue rotting away until nothing remains.

A deep growl echoes between the walls before the sound eventually absorbs in the crevices holding every stone in place. Did George forget to bring me food again? Another night without a plate, a bowl, a morsel, a crumb of food. Pork, chicken, a loaf of bread, or even an apple would suffice. Oh, those were the days! Dish after dish, meal after meal with no one to share it with, aside from Teddy, I suppose.

The whine of the floorboards beneath my feet jolts me back to the harsh reality of my room now. No food sits on the desk like there usually is, but a yellow folder rests on top of the stack of papers littering the desk. A new case! The chair groans like an old basset hound walking on its weary old bones as I pull it out, the mahogany back smooth in the palm of my hand.

A man was found in the river, drowned and bloated. A young adult with blond hair and blue eyes, nothing out of the ordinary. Perhaps someone shoved him. Maybe he jumped. There are no bruises or markings, except for a star-shaped birthmark on his neck; nothing indicates any reason for foul play. This case will collect dust as the others fly off the shelf.

A star-shaped birthmark? It can't be! My mind flies back to the file from years ago. There were no traces and only a star-shaped birthmark on his neck as an identifier.

What are the chances? George will be so impressed! But first, I need to verify this is not a coincidence. All the old folders from old cases are housed upstairs in the common area for the other constables. Within view of any potential late-night workers. Should I? Yes. This is the only way to know for sure; if all the object descriptions match, this could be enough to solve his disappearance after all this time. Perhaps even enough to give George the power to promote me to an actual position, working a job, and making a wage, instead of spending sleepless nights silently solving cases in exchange for a place to live.

I make my way up the stairs, and I have to allow time for my eyes to adjust to the darkness. Relying on memory, I dance through the hallways, weaving gracefully between all the obstacles as I have roamed these halls in secret for years. Long enough to spark ghost stories about that whispering woman through the walls, the ghost of Scotland Yard who spends her nights obsessing over the case no one could solve, muttering the words on the files, searching in hopes of finding the one she seeks. Although these tales are quite outdated, I stopped whispering while I read quite some time ago. I no longer need the practice; I can read on my own.

Finally! In the third-floor collections room, the file has to be here somewhere. Yet, what was the name of that poor boy? Vincent? No, that doesn't seem right. Philip isn't right, either. Peter? Peter! His name was Peter, though there is no hope of remembering his last name. That will remain a mystery, as his disappearance has been all these years.

The wooden floorboards under foot creak with every step. Along the way, I pass several desks for other constables. The trail leads up to the door of the venerated Chief, George Hudson. Dread fills me as my hand rests on the doorknob that shares the same icy exterior as the brass entryway gates of the property. A series of formidable filing cabinets line up in front of me inside the doors, waiting for me to open them and reveal their secrets of forgotten cases, wishing for someone to breathe life into their names once again. I guess there is no better place to start than the beginning.

A piercing scream stabs my ears as I yank the first drawer from the socket with enough vigor to topple the whole cabinet. Flipping through every bluc envelope, I catch a glimpse of every forgotten person, every forgotten story, tucked away into a metal coffin, never to see the light of day again. I can't help but feel a twinge of remorse for these people. Can I do more? Should I be doing more?

While completing this mindless task, I let my thoughts run free, conjuring a list of things to do tonight before going back into seclusion for the morning. Although there is undoubtedly other work to be done, this is all I intend to finish. Teddy will be happy to be able to see me again. If I can find Peter's case soon, the two of us will have almost the entire night together, just like in the old days.

Peter! Yes, this is him! Peter Acker, a child who disappeared when he was twelve years old, has blond hair, blue eyes, and a star-shaped birthmark on his neck. The drawer grumbles as I shove it back, pulling the file before the dull thud echoes through the stone walls.

Glancing up, I come face to face with the boy sharing the same likeness as the old profile in my hand describes, down to the birthmark. I take one step back, but he stays in the same spot.

"Peter?" I ask, unsure of what else to ask this child.

He nods his head but says nothing.

"Did you hear that?" a man whispers from the hallway.

A mutter of agreement passes through the group passing the threshold and into the room. I have no choice but to hide against the filing cabinet as Peter blurs from view. I am out of sight for now. But I can't stay crouched here forever. Where did Peter go? Where do I go now? They will all see me if I run before I reach the door. If I remain here, they will find me when they leave. I'm doomed if I stay and doomed if I escape.

I peek over the side of the metal box to see who is there and see four men in the station's uniforms loiter around the desks, fumbling to find their tools. The leader glances at his fellow detectives, ordering them to only take what they need. His eyes are quite odd, one is blue, and the other is hazel. He jerks his head in my direction, and I throw my neck back behind the safety of the cabinet.

"Gentlemen, we have no time to waste," his voice booms, looking back to his men. "Grab your equipment. We must leave straight away."

"Why do we need to answer this call so late?" a voice whines.

"The sooner we get to the Yeats's home and inspect the murder, the sooner we can get home." His gruff voice echoes through the room. "But we have to do this now before the girl finds herself buried in one of these cabinets."

A child? Another murder? As the years have passed, that string of words never gets easier to hear.

The soft pattering of footsteps fills the hallway, abruptly stopping upon entering the room. "Ann, are you here?"

Teddy. On no. What is he doing here?

"Ann?" he calls, poking his head in through the door, coming face to face with all the other constables in the room.

"Who are you?" one demands.

"How did you get in here? You shouldn't be allowed in!" another constable yells.

"Who is Ann? Is she in here, too?"

Chairs scrape against the floor, followed by rustling as the men frantically move around the room, trying to find me.

"I truly apologize, constables. I must have the wrong room." A dry laugh escapes as Teddy tries to ease the tension in the room. "I'll just see myself out."

"You're not going anywhere! Men, stop him!" their leader booms.

Now is as good a chance as any. I pick up my skirts, clutching the file tightly, and run through the door I entered, grabbing Teddy's arm as I release my dresses on the way out.

There is nothing more on my mind than running.

"She's the ghost, men! She's real!" I hear behind me, followed by the heavy thudding of their boots as they follow us out the door. I scurry away back into the depths of the streets and waste no time leaving the premises with the files in hand. I proceed with haste to the Yeats's house, not wasting a precious moment because I cannot afford it.

"Darling, where are we going?" Teddy questions.

"Away." I gasp between strides. "There is a case I might be able to help with."

"You still wish to continue this madness, dear? You still want to work for these detectives after everything?"

"Especially after everything," I counter. "Shut up and keep running!"

"Darling, you know very well that is not possible." He laughs before it's drowned out by the light clamor of the city life at night as we cross the street to get to the well-known Yeats house.

Throngs of people stand outside the property of the esteemed Yeats' manor, hoping to get a glimpse of this elusive family between the bars. The gates are closed, warding off any ill-intended visitors until tonight. The ghouls of grief run rampant through the grass, attracting the eyes of those who wish to prey off the wails seeping from this mournful house for nothing more than a shred of gossip.

Creaking and squeaking abruptly greet my ear as the gate opens for the black carriage, beckoning me inside this walled fortress alongside this familiar vessel. Hiding behind the back wall of this vehicle rolling through the entryway, I sneak in. The ornately forged gates close behind me before anyone else can slither their way in. The cast iron bars are decorated with ivy branches that spiral and point at the top to keep unwanted visitors away, but the thieving vultures will stop at nothing tonight to get a single morsel to take home with them.

I am transported to the day of my father's funeral as I sit facing the driver, waiting for George to return and take his place opposite of me as he did that day, and again the day he drove me home back home. The carriage comes to a jarring halt at the front door, and before the man inside opens, I push the door and throw myself inside, knowing exactly who it is and that only he can fix this problem. The door howls as it opens, followed by the loud squeaks as George is frantic in his actions to get in and close the door rapidly.

"Are you stupid, child? What are you doing here?" he demands. "You know our arrangement. It could be dangerous if someone sees you!"

"I assure you, no one saw me, sir," I plead to the darkness. "But you have to let me help with this case!"

"Believe it or not, I share this sentiment."

A smile lightens the weight on my chest as I feel happy at this moment.

"But do not start celebrating yet, my dear. I'm afraid it comes with a catch."

No. Why is there always a catch?

"There have been far too many sightings of you recently, and I cannot keep this matter quiet any longer—"

"I know I left the basement, and I will try to limit my excursions. But sir, tonight I solved an old case from a file upstairs."

A friend that is truly happy to usher in the successes of another. The sides of his handlebar mustache lift as he smiles. "My child," he says slowly, "I can't keep protecting you. You've gone too far this time, and I can't save you. The deal I made to your father expired long ago. There is nothing I can do for you if you refuse to obey simple orders!"

"But where will I go? I have no home," I plead, "I have no money, no family. I love what I do and want to continue helping the city. I always have! Can't you find me a job?" I am talking to keep my thoughts at bay and the words keep falling from my mouth without much thought. "You're the captain. You can make me a constable!"

"You know it does not work like that," he begins. "There is no way others will let you keep that position for long, and it's my head they'll come after once they discard you."

"But there has to be something you can do, right? What about this case I solved? Isn't this enough to convince them?" I say, dejected and deflated.

"Unfortunately, dear, that alone will not suf-fice… But the murder of little Delia Yeats might be enough."

"What are you saying? Will they let me work with them?"

"Not quite." He strikes a match and begins puffing on his pipe. "If you can find the murderer of a member of such a prominent family as the Yeats, they may be more inclined to help you, even per-suade the officials to get you a job on the force."

A position as a constable, at long last! This brief elation is quickly hit by the heavy blow of reality, and soon after, doubt settles in my mind, feeding at my tranquility, growing uncertainty.

"I will give you one day to find who is responsi-ble for this crime. You know as well as I do that once that window closes, it is unlikely the murderer will be found. If you can't meet this deadline, you will be dismissed. Permanently."

Permanently. The word rings through my head, bouncing from one side to the other with no other thoughts to slow its pace. "But sir, that's not nearly enough time. Besides, how will I find evidence if they are unaware I am on the case?"

"These are not my problems. My debt to your family expired long ago. You have twenty-four hours, or I shall see to it you are arrested for trespassing should I find the ghost of Scotland Yard sleeping in the basement again." He looks at me before continu-ing. "I truly am sorry, but there is nothing more I can do."

"Please, sir, just a few more days." I am compromising my beliefs in begging, but the fear of being evicted weighs far heavier on my chest. "Let me finish out this week," I plead, disappointed at my tone.

"Ann, I cannot honor that request." He nods, as if agreeing with his own assessment. "I must warn you... it is truly harrowing inside. To see the body of a twelve-year-old like that..." His eyes flit to the window, but I can see a single tear reflecting off his cheek in the moonlight. "I should advise you it is imperative you set your emotions aside in this case. They cannot get involved in trying to solve the murder of such a young child; it will drive you to insanity. There is not much evidence, and I am not sure I need to remind you of the Yeats family and their connections throughout the city. It needs to be carried out quickly and quietly."

*Click, click, click.* The steady sound of footsteps grows nearer to the carriage door.

"I told you to be careful!" Hudson whispers. "Someone noticed you! Quick, leave before they see!"

Opening the door, he gestures for me to jump from the side door, and the cloud of smoke from his pipe blankets me. My foot meets the cobblestone driveway as I throw myself from the door. I slam it just before the hinges squeak like the other door. I hide my face from the world, crouching underneath the glass, but I am stuck. The hem of my petticoats remains tightly locked in the jaws of the door. The night sky will mask my presence, though; it always does.

# Chapter Eight

## 21 January 1901

"Is there something I can help you with, Chief?" a woman's voice asks inside the carriage.

"No, Ms. Yeats, but I appreciate your concern," Hudson responds.

"I would appreciate it if you would move your carriage off of our property." The frost from her voice passes through the door. "You are blocking traffic into the house."

"Of course. I will leave straight away, Ms. Yeats," he complies.

"And I hope I do not need to remind you of our confidentiality agreement," she fumes before slamming the door.

The click of her heels resumes again as she walks back into the house. I have enough time to yank my skirts from the door as the carriage drives off into the night.

The Yeats are certainly not the wealthiest family in the city; however, their house is a luxury I could only dream of having anymore. I turn my head toward the house and am struck by the stunning building that the night sky still partially shrouds. Anguish rests atop the house, but it has an endearing quality. The house is stoic, wearing the grief but still radiating the elegance and charm of the family. The pale stone exterior accents the dark rooftops. The gothic structure has two triangle shapes in the front, with two large windows, allowing them to stare at the world passing them by as they remain trapped behind the glass fortress.

A howling moan strikes me through my heart, freezing all emotion until there is no choice but for me to wade through this grief. The River of Styx that has flooded this house. One step. Two steps. On the third step, I pass the threshold, the point of no return, and the door shuts behind me, latching as it seals any view of the outside world out of sight.

There is nothing but a carpeted set of stairs in front of me, dividing the house into two wings. Doors line the hallways as far as I can see down either path. Wails and soft murmurs pour out the door, thick as molasses, trying to trap any unsuspecting prey in its sticky arms. There is not a soul in the lower body of the house, for all the life has flocked to the heart of this tragedy, giving one last breath to the room of the dead child.

I listen to the sound of the wails, hesitant to see the ugly face of this monstrous grief, reluctant to be seen and dismissed as nothing more than a vulture hoping to find a single morsel of gossip to bring back to the committee. Not one step creaks or groans underfoot as I move up the house, clutching the banister, desperately trying not to get caught in the torrential waves of grief pouring down the staircase.

As I near the top, the pathway branches into two separate hallways, each adorned with an emerald damask wallpaper and several oil lanterns clinging to the walls, just as below. Their faint gold glow emerging from the glass covers lights the path, allowing me to see oak doorways lining both sides of the hall. All are closed, except for the one closest to the right. Candlelight spills on the floor, and obsidian figures dance their mournful tune as they pass by each light and darken outside the room.

"My baby!" The woman's wails in a white nightgown stop my blood in its veins. "My baby, my baby. Who did this? Look at what they've done!"

A child lies on the ground with nothing but her mother's legs to rest on; her mother's white gown soaks up her scarlet blood spilling on the carpet. The crimson life oozing from the gaping hole in the child's chest leeches on the cotton nightgown, but nothing can collect the youthfulness and store it until the child can breathe again.

Another figure kneels opposite of the mother, holding the girl's hand, muttering words only meant for his sister.

"Please," the whisper echoes through the room. "Delia, please. Please come back!" He calls her name, but there is only silence. He pleads for his mother's support, but there are only wails. The youthful vigor that once bound down the hallways will remain as stiff as the girl's corpse.

The five of them stand huddled together, unmoving, unspeaking, and if I didn't know any better, unbreathing. The mother is wrapped around her child's body, the victim's hand is grasped tightly in her older brother's, while the eldest son rests one hand on each of his brother's and mother's shoulders, perhaps offering some form of comfort while her sister stands behind them, completing the picture while remaining distant.

"Addie," a third figure calls, beckoning the woman dissociating herself from the spectacle on the floor. "Addie, you know she would—"

"She is dead, Abraham!" she spits at the other figure. "You could not possibly know what she would want!"

"No, no, no…" The mother's shrieks continue one right after the other as no other sound can dismiss the reality at hand.

"Addie, she's our sister. Our baby sister!"

"Please excuse me, brother." Her words are curt and sharp as a blow. "I am feeling quite unwell and wish to leave."

"Adelaide—" But she is no longer in the room after her brother gets her name out.

The blood rushes to my head, drawing out the sound of the mother's sobs. I can feel my legs twitch, reminding me to move, but I am not sure I want to. I had to do something. Where do I go? Where can I hide? What should I do? Thoughts flood my head, and I am paralyzed, unable to decide how to disappear as Addie gets one step closer to me, closer to casting me off before I even have a chance. I trudge through the invisible wave of hands pulling me back until I reach the door nearest me on the opposite side of the corridor from the child's room. Surely no one has locked it amid this commotion. A squeal lets out as the bedroom door opens, and light pours into the hallway, erasing the obsidian figures wallowing in this grief. A calm, collected footstep, one at a time, graces the floorboards until they stop abruptly. Before I close the door, hiding away in this mysterious room, I can hear her voice again.

"Constables, I would like to speak with you again about the matter we discussed earlier. How do you plan on ensuring my family's privacy regarding this incident?"

Click. The door closes, and I am no longer part of their conversation.

The latch catching in the door frame echoes, as it is the only sound in the room. The silence is deafening, and I suspect this is what it is like in a casket six feet underground.

How will I solve this before the nighttime comes along tomorrow? Where will I go? Who will take me in? What have I done to make Hudson turn on me? Why did I do this?

Books. The smell interrupts my marathon of thoughts—it is one smell that I would recognize anywhere. Books. Rows and rows of books live here. This room must be a vast library, full of treasures from the minds of others bold enough to write them down. Paper and ink mixed with dust fill my lungs, and I am happy. My heart leaps at the sight of paper basking in the starlight seeping in from the giant paned window along the back wall. The stars are the only source of light, glimmering softly through the windows. All the furniture and details of the room are absorbed by the night's darkness; I am left to guess what else this room holds. If I light a candle, the flame will seep into the hallway, and I will be found. If I make any noise, they'll discover my secret plot. So, silently I sit in the darkness, piecing together the nature of this foul crime under the guidance of my own thoughts. This differs only slightly from the many nights spent under the guise of candlelight in my home library. Although, the sound of Teddy's voice whispering throughout the night has now replaced the sound of my own thoughts bickering amongst each other.

A string of lanterns line the walls; each flicker casts the shadows away for a brief moment before being swallowed by the darkness. The quivering flame reveals a clue, and I can see I am no longer in the Yeats' house. I am at my own home. My old one, that is, the one that died in the fire, along with a piece of my soul as I saw the life I knew crumble with the ashes and dissolve into the soil. And so this delicate dance continues and shall continue for the end of time; a dance of life amidst the troubling darkness.

The years have withered out of my grasp, leaving nothing more than wisps of sand blowing away into the wind, but I would recognize this library anywhere. I am no longer standing on the second floor of the Yeats' manor. Instead, for a brief moment in my mind, I stand shrouded in the embrace of the library from my childhood home, and it is good to be back in the arms of an old friend. I am not an orphaned rat dwelling with the rest of the vermin in the shadows beneath the streets. I am home.

As quick as it came on, the crushing weight resting upon my chest from the immeasurable burden of this case comes crashing back down, suffocating me in the rubble of my broken bones. The only way to clear away the wreckage is to solve this murder, which is the cause of the destruction. It is quite ironic how the source of this pain is the only medicine to alleviate it. I have no time to hide in the past. As much as I wish it weren't true, I cannot go back home; I can never sit in the familiar hug of that old friend. There is no point in waltzing through these memories only to be run into the tombstone of what lay buried.

Perhaps I should leave before anyone notices. I could go now; no one else would know of this ludicrous plan to find this murderer. How could I solve this? Me? No, it is not possible. Although, I am certain the cockiness of the constables swarming this house prevents them from finding all the clues.

No. I need to leave. This is not my responsibility. It is not my place to be observing such private emotions. I feel my surroundings, careful not to bump into the furniture leading up to the windows. If the panes let me out, I can crawl through them and run away into the night without anyone noticing. I glance out the window and my blood runs cold as I see a figure attempting to squeeze through the iron bars of the gates.

Teddy. I would recognize him anywhere. He will be arrested with witnesses to bear their testimony to his crime! What is he trying to do?

I push down on the copper handles. The windows are open, and the breeze from outside brushes through my hair. He is truly mad! I have to stop him! But the child's sister is standing by the only exit, completing her duty to direct newly arriving constables and coroners on the property. It is impossible to escape unnoticed. If I try to stop Teddy, I risk both of our captures. There is nothing for me to do but remain here until the family retires for the night. But how long would that be? It could be hours from now. The Yeats would need the rest of the night to patch pieces of the floor that had shattered underneath their unsuspecting feet.

A little body snuffed out by the sharp blade of cruelty rests a mere few hundred feet from me, and despite my wishes, there is nothing to be done to restore this house to its original state. But if I can find the murderer, perhaps I can aid in healing the poorly sutured gashes.

There will be no other constable to scrutinize my work. My heart soars at this revelation. I feel free at last. Free in my own decisions, an endless list of choices. Where do I start? Is one option truly better than the other? Where do I begin looking? What am I even looking for? I suppose I am searching for something waiting to be found.

I creep to the door once again despite the hammering of my heart advising me to choose another plan, a safer one. The hinges let out a slight squeal as I open the door just enough to let me see out into the hallway. But I hear the mother before anything else.

"My baby… my baby, my baby…" She continues murmuring to herself, as there is no one nearby able to understand her loss or help her to hold the heavy weight of a small child in her arms.

The mother cannot contain her emotions any more than the ocean can contain its waves in the midst of a storm. Horses carry their cargo in the streets, and the moon continues beaming on the world below, but this moment will be frozen in time eternally for the Yeats. The source of their youth has been robbed, brutally ripped away from them in the dark of the night.

The family will have to endure this pain for the remainder of their days because there is no cure to fix their wounds. Nothing can be done to bring back the dead, and there is no comfort in knowing anything more can grow from this tragedy.

The wails seep down the walls, trapping anyone who dares to listen to the tragic tune of a mother forced to live out her days without her baby. I am stuck in this net and I cannot leave this house before I have searched every nook and cranny. This song should never be played again. No mother should have to utter these horrid lyrics, and no sibling should have to listen to these laments.

The hallway is empty, so I take one silent step on the red carpet and scurry to the end of the corridor to find a room to throw myself into before being spotted.

My eyes adjust to the darkness. The slight flicker of a candle in the corner of the room is enough to see the contents inside. I'm not sure what I expected. Perhaps a glamorous display of family wealth, but that is certainly not what I see. There is nothing more than the bare necessities in this room. A large bed rests against the far wall in the center of the room. A nightstand sits on each side of the bed, and a long dresser stretches across a large portion of the wall next to the doorway. A collection of pebbles, shells, and pressed flowers lies on this wooden cabinet. Portraits of the silhouettes of their children are displayed as a testament to the life this family built for themselves. One child lines up after the other as they progress in age, the resemblance is uncanny, but I suppose now the smallest one will remain forever unaltered.

The inside of the room is relatively scant and devoid of embellishments and frills. Perhaps they choose to spend their time in other areas of the house, the library or gardens. There are many duties to fulfill each day to keep them away from their rooms.

I rummage through the drawers and find nothing but their clothes. Their bedside tables offer nothing but space to hold a single book and oil lamp.

The door opens without a sound, and the hallway is empty once more, so I exit from where I came from and hurry to the next door.

The door screams at me to turn away as the unoiled hinges hesitantly grant the door permission to swing open. The shadows within make it difficult to distinguish any object, but I can see a sliver of moonlight peeking through a crack on the wall directly opposite me. There are no candles and no lamps that offer any opportunity to see what lies inside. Opening the curtains would be my only hope of seeing anything. I place one foot into the room, and the tendrils of the night begin creeping up my leg. It slithers around the floor, waiting to claim another victim, swallowing them whole before they know what has happened. I close my eyes and run straight across the room with my hand outstretched until I feel the thick, smooth, silky curtain in the palm of my hand. I throw open the drapes, and the white rays from the moon in the sky floods into the room, bathing the darkness in its rich liquor. Finally, I can see!

Standing in front of me is a bed, perfectly made, with four posts stationed on each corner. There is a plain bedspread, which pairs nicely with the ornate mahogany bed frame. The poles are decorated with intricate designs, each as unique as the last. The grooves dance across my fingertips, painting a story on my skin as I run my fingers over them. Various floral families playfully interact with letters that work together to create an image.

I turn my eyes away from the posts as I remember the necessity of finding something, yet I hope there is nothing here that will incriminate anyone inside the house. I still believe no member of the Yeats' would have been able to commit this abhorrent crime against one of their own, yet I suppose others would need convincing.

Resting directly across from the foot of the bed is an organized desk covered in a thick film of dust; not a single piece of paper is out of place. Rummaging through the drawers offers no help. Receipts, short pieces of prose, and more dust are the only contents aside from the tools that created them. Further down the wall stands an armoire, identical to the one in the other room and devoid of clues.

There are no other items for me to search through, and an empty floor under the bed depletes me of any hope of finding anything that could be used to identify the murderer. The bedspread wrinkles under me as I sit on the edge of the mattress.

What will I do now? How am I to solve this case if I cannot find a clue or trait of the killer? What am I even looking for? My time is running out, and Hudson has already grown tired of my failures. It is only a matter of time before… I need to find something. I must.

The stiff fabric of my petticoats does not move against the palm of my hands as I run them down my sides in an effort to clear the perspiration and stabilize them before resting them on my lap.

I suppose all I can do now is take the next step out of this room and into another—that terrifying step into the empty chasm of uncertainty—for I do not know if I will find anything of value before being caught. Step by step, I make my way to the door until I find myself staring at the face of yet another entryway in the same corridor.

I rest my hand on the door handle, unsure if I should proceed further. There's a tugging at my gut as I cannot help but feel I am trespassing. These people are already haunted by the ghouls of remorseful reminiscence. I do not wish to add to their heartbreak on this night of betrayal. Grief has struck this family down with the force of a storm at sea, rocking their ship and inspiring fear of capsizing. As they sway amidst the winds of change and lay bare beneath the torrential tears pouring upon them, the Yeats have no choice but to calm the maelstrom raging around them. In a time unkind to all, the family has been given little alternative than secluding themselves, leaving the public to wonder what is occurring behind their closed doors. I suspect their iron gates will remain firmly locked forever, stopping reality from snatching away another one of their children in the dark.

I push down on the handle and take a step inside, but to my surprise, the bright flame from the lamp on the bedside table lights up the room, and I am greeted by lines creating playful drawings covering the entirety of the inside of the room. No matter where I turn, I see beautiful expressions, which is a welcome change from the other chambers devoid of personalization. Every inch of space is covered by a square of paper imprinted with faces, buildings, garden flowers, wildlife, or other peculiar, indistinct shapes. They arch around the vanity mirror along the wall opposite the bed, flooding the blank space on either side of this sole piece of furniture. They go to the top of the room, lining the ceiling across the bare walls, and line each side of the bed. The depth behind every stroke is astounding and tells the story of unkempt emotion. Violent strokes of the pencil and tortured lines of pages resting in disarray on top of the dresser convey the grief and turmoil wrestling within this person. It is evident that the expression of whomever this bedroom belongs to is confined to these drawings. These must have taken months, even years to draw.

I force myself to look away, to focus my eyes on any other portion of this room and find it is not much for me to look through. I begin my search, glancing through the dresser, the vanity, and the small bookshelf peeking out from the corner adjacent to the bed. However, there is nothing there. Again.

I slowly peek out the door, waiting to ensure there would be no witnesses on the other side of the door. Voices fill the hallway, and I whip my head back into the room but keep the door slightly open, so I can hear what is being said.

"I must thank you again, constables," the voice says. "For all you have done for my family. My mother and brothers are retiring for the night. I will show you out, and I suppose I should follow suit."

And now, the room of this vile crime lies as empty as the unmarked tomb of a forgotten person centuries after their demise. The girl's room is next door, and I know I have no choice but to disturb the place of little Delia Yeats' last breath if I wish to have any luck finding who did this. Each stride to her doorway brings me closer to peering into her final moments and I grow weary of the thought of such a personal disturbance.

The hallway is barren, except for the candle-light lining it, which illuminates the green damask wallpaper. The wails remain in the air in place of the wooden planks on the floor, seeping through the splinters of the white door, the one belonging to a child who would never step foot in this room again.

The door stares at me, waiting for me to open it so it can reveal all of its secrets, but I cannot bring myself to continue. I lightly push on the door to open it. The silent screech of the hinges greets my ears while I turn the knob as if warning Cordelia of someone trying to unearth her secret. Everything else around me is unimportant. None of it can save me from the cold, looming threat of the guillotine hanging above my neck; only what lies on the other side of this door can. I turn the handle, but before I take my first step, I stand in the doorway, hoping someone will push me in. Right as I decide to cross into the room, a hand shoves me inside.

I whip my head back to see who is responsible for pushing me, only to come face to face with the door. It is only me. I creep inside the room at my new surroundings, and the room seems so painfully familiar for a moment. My heart sings, skipping beats in sync with the melody. The golden haze of frozen time encompasses all the child's belongings, and the rays dance before my eyes.

# Chapter Nine

## 21 January 1901

My eyes glaze over the contents present directly in front of me, my heart sinks a little. Here lies the grave of a child. Her body no longer lingers on the floor, but her soul remains forever attached to these four walls. The blood no longer pools at the base of the bed, but the essence of her life seeps through the rug and across the floorboards. In the dresses in her drawers, the jewelry resting next to her bed, and the drawings sprawled on her desk, I can see proof of the life she breathed and of the life that exists no more.

My eyes immediately focus on the stained carpet, to the spot that soaked up the last bit of life. There is nothing more than a stain to commemorate this tragic loss, nothing that can be used to find who did this. I need to spend my time looking elsewhere, but I must force myself to turn away from that spot.

I yank open the first drawer in her dresser, feeling through her dresses, hoping there is something hidden between the folds or evidence of theft, but my fingers tap against the bottom. I begin to push the drawer back in, but after a moment, I realize something quite peculiar. It is not bursting with her garments; in fact, there are very few. Could the murderer have stolen her clothes before fleeing? But her pearl necklace and diamond earrings remain on her bedside table. Perhaps money was not the objective.

I carefully examine the contents of her nightstand, but nothing irregular appears. Nothing is out of place. Frustration begins gnawing at my naïve optimism, because there is nothing else worth exploring.

As I near the door, I turn around for one last glance to find that the rug's corner folded under itself. Could such a fine home still have loose floorboards? A strategically placed rug could hide this. Of course, I'd know this. As quickly as it came on, the frustration leaves and my hope restores as I kneel down. I pull the rug aside as a coroner peels back the layers of the heart in an autopsy. A nail slightly pokes its head out from the wooden plank below it. I lift it from its home before moving to the next one. The pins lie on the floor as I pry the floorboard up, revealing a glimmer of yellow. My heart sings, skipping a beat at this find. I move to the last board and begin again until I stare into a square pit.

The cold clings to my hand as I stick it into the hole. Laying in front of me is a white leather suitcase with a gold handle and the letters "AY" engraved on the top. Grasping the gold object, I pull it out and place it on the bed.

AY? Her family called her Cordelia, Delia, earlier. Is this hers?

I push up on the latches on the side of it, and the hard-shell case releases, exposing its contents. Directly on top of all the folded dresses lay a boat ticket to America with the name "Alexandra Cordelia Yeats" written in bold letters. The child must've gone by her middle name.

Cordelia was planning on running away. Her clothes are all packed, and there is only a single ticket; she had no intention of returning. Rummaging through the rest of her suitcase, I find nothing else but clothes. I stare in disbelief at the paper. The departure date is only a few short hours away. There is no sound aside from the whistling of the wind outside and the tree branches tapping the windows.

I put the ticket down, walk over to the window, and see the small pools of water resting on the cobblestone road between the buildings crammed together, reflecting the streetlight. The tapping is just the tree branches, nothing more.

A flash outside draws my attention to the gates; a figure attempts to wiggle its way through the barricade. Teddy. His shadow melts into a puddle and spills between the bars until he takes form on the other side of the gate. Why is he coming back?

I fling the latches open, hoist up my skirts as I prepare to jump down without a second thought. He successfully passed through the gate, and so now I have no choice but to launch myself from the room. The soft earth sinks under my feet as I stand straight before rushing over to him. I pass a great, sturdy apple tree along the way, with flexed roots, prepared to trap and trip anyone bold enough to step on its fingers. I stop in my tracks and notice the familiar red vest in front of me beneath the sanctuary of the branches. He glances down in the bushes as if he is looking for something, unaware of my presence.

Teddy. How stupid could he be? If anyone sees him here, if he is not careful, he could destroy everything I have built so far. The ground squelches underfoot as I march toward him, and with each aggressive tap on his shoulder, I transport back to the same thuds on my door years ago. The same blazer that greeted me at the door that day stares me in the eyes as I aggressively tap his arm in the shadows of a stranger's property.

"What are you doing here?" Each word leaves my mouth harsher than intended.

"Ann, I told you I would help you in this case," Teddy stammers as he slowly turns around, putting his hands up. "I've been waiting outside the gates since you arrived, or have you forgotten already?"

"No!" I exclaim before I can even process what he is saying. "You were here earlier and did us all a favor by leaving! Why did you come back?"

"This is not quite the warm welcome I anticipated." He chuckles. "But I would like to help!"

"I have to do this on my own, and I am on a very tight deadline and don't need any distractions." I gesture to him. "Gone."

"Deadline?"

"I have until tomorrow to find out who did this."

"Tomorrow!" He laughs. "You know as well as I do that is impossible! Why would you agree?"

"Because it's my only option," I say, defeated. "If I cannot, I will have to find a new place to live."

"But… your home is here. Where else could you move? Who else would take you in?"

"No one! That is why I need you to leave, so I can figure this out and…" the words lodge in the back of my throat, not wanting to utter the words of defeat, "not be kicked into the streets, like that old lady we saw all those years ago. What about your cousin? Can we visit him?"

"What old lady? Besides, I have already told you, that is—"

"Not an option. I know!" I snap, completing his sentence for him. "Why can we not go?"

"The journey to his house is too dangerous of a trek. It's not worth the risk. Besides, my only family would not be happy to see us on a random afternoon after years of no contact. Us being unmarried would not be doing us any favors as well."

"I'm not getting married yet! I still have time to fix this before I give away what little freedoms I have left! You have to go so I can go back inside!"

Surely there must be some excuse we can concoct to give a reason to visit his family! He saw the old lady as I did all those years ago. Was that image not enough to show him what would become of me if I am not careful? Does he not want to help me? There are only so many reasons to thwart every credible plan of mine…

"I have nothing else to do outside of these gates. Ann, you do not want to do this… I am only helping you, and you would be wrong to refuse my services.

I am the only person offering it right now, and you know as well as I that you need all of the help you can get if you don't want to end up homeless," he says. "Again."

I suppose there is no harm in enlisting one more person in my efforts to find the killer. After all, Hudson never said I couldn't ask others for their input. All the other constables have each other to ask. Why should I not be privy to that same privilege?

"Oh, all right." A slight smirk turns up at the corner of my mouth. "But only for a few minutes! I do not know how much longer I have before anyone inside leaves their rooms."

"We must begin working immediately. Do you have any theories, or are you already further behind?"

With every breath, the ticking of the clock grows louder, closer to striking two-twenty-two. The coldness of his voice echoes, yet his eagerness to learn the details remind me of an excited schoolboy. Although I take great offense to his condescending attitude, I know he is right. If I cannot find anything to point me in the right direction, I am doomed.

"I found a suitcase full of clothes hidden under her bed and a ticket to America."

He waits a moment before responding, "Is that it?"

"What is that supposed to mean? I have made as much progress as possible with what little I have been given!"

"What progress? From what I have gathered, there is nothing to analyze," he booms.

"Be quiet, or you will wake them!" I hiss, ducking away from the view of any of the windows. "It has only been a few hours since this case started… how on earth do you expect me to have found anything more?"

He lets out a long sigh. "I suppose. Do you think there is a possibility it was self-inflicted?"

"I am positive it was not something she did of her own volition. I suspect the murderer hunted only Cordelia. He had no other motive. Whoever murdered her knew and targeted her. The ticket to America indicates she had plans for the near future. I do not think she would kill herself before going. There is nothing proving she may have wanted to do so. Besides, the viciousness with which the knife was plunged into her chest could not have been done by herself. It was buried in her ribcage; there is no way someone such as her would have the strength to do that to themselves."

"But have you considered the possibility that someone in the family—"

"No!" My curt response comes off more aggressive than intended, but only I was there to witness their reactions. No one else can understand the raw, unfiltered emotion that passed through me like a ghost earlier. "The Yeats would never kill one of their own!"

"You would be wise to consider this," he begins. "People can put on realistic masks and adopt these personalities. Cordelia and her family are not exempt from this. Do not be so quick to dismiss the theory."

"However," I counter, "I believe it was someone who knew her because there is no other evidence elsewhere in the house. Nothing was taken, and she was the only one targeted. If this was a random killing, the murderer would have stolen from the family to get some sort of profit. Or they would have tried to murder someone else. Instead, he knew to enter through Cordelia's window. The bottom floor would have been easier to sneak through." I take a few steps back, dragging Teddy with me to show him where I jumped from. "Look, Teddy, the plants here are smashed down from repetitive stomping. This is directly beneath her window. Someone inside or outside repetitively stood here or jumped down on this spot."

"Do you know what her relationship with this person was?"

"No, and that is where I am stuck. This is where I need your help the most. However, I think she was sneaking out to meet people. I think she escaped from her window to escape the gates."

"Was there anyone else around the property you could have questioned? Someone who could have indicated where the killer went?"

A rock starts forming in my throat. I should have asked other people. I should have walked around the premises first. I should have—

"Are you seriously not able to answer this question as well? Must I solve the case for you? The ticket to America is your clue!"

"How?" It is the only word I manage to utter as I have shrunk into my body, becoming half my size. I should be able to ask and answer these questions myself, much less without the help of someone with no experience. After all, this is my job, not his.

"You cannot be serious. The evidence is directly in front of you! If she sneaked out to meet these people whom her family is unaware of, we could assume she sneaked people inside, too. She would not dare bring anyone in or out during the daytime; the chances of being caught would be too high. She would only sneak someone in at night, but only someone she would deem worthy of taking that risk. Someone she cared very deeply for. Someone she could run away with."

It was so obvious, but I missed it. Perhaps this case should be in someone else's hands.

"You're a better detective than this," he scolds, disappointed.

Now I am the schoolchild, waiting to be chastised for something I did not do, yet the feeling of guilt and apprehension weigh heavily on my chest.

"I think it is time for me to go back in and try to find more clues supporting our new theory." Each word sinks me further into this sea of self-dejection. He takes one step with me, and I know what he is attempting. I lightly place my hand on his shoulder to stop him. "I believe they would not like to have yet another stranger in their house."

"But I would like to do something. I would like to think they want all the help they can get," he pleads. "Please, it will give me something to do!"

A single shake of my head is enough for him to understand.

Teddy is disgruntled by this response, but he complies nonetheless. "I will need you to close the gates from the inside when I go out. You do not want to let anyone else in tonight. The murderer may come back," he grumbles.

"I'll walk with you," I say, hoping to clear his frustration.

With each step, my stomach sinks further down, as if the walls of support that once stood there have turned to quicksand. My surroundings blur around me as I continue this dreaded hike. I can feel bombs blasting on my self-confidence and self-esteem, obliterating the hope I have for a better future and for justice. Each step up is like one step down in the ocean, willingly beckoning me into its depths to suck the air from my lungs. How will I ever solve this? Alone?

"Darling, when will I see you again?" he turns to ask before walking through the bars.

"Meet at the end of the street at sunrise, and we can talk later," I say, shutting the gate, separating the two of us for now.

The hinges squeal as I close them, and I worry it is loud enough to disturb the Yeats as they mourn inside. Once the latch catches, I could feel my inner peace dissipate, as if the closing of the door severed a piece of me. Yet, now I am on my own, I cannot help but lose myself in my thoughts over this case. I face a tide that pulls me under each time I think of another task I have to accomplish to get answers. The more I think of this murder, the more my hopes are dashed. I feel a hitch in my breath and find that my breaths are far shallower than before. I shake my head, clearing it of the fog that seeped into it through the madness.

Alone, I trek the path again to Cordelia's bedroom. The solitude from the short walk offers me solace and I can breathe again at last. How on earth am I to get back up through her window? There is nothing for me to grab or climb up against the flat wall of the house's side. The doors are indeed locked now. Although…

An idea takes shape in my mind. Even though this pillar is not directly under her window, it can lead me to the slanted roof above, which is a jump away from her room. It's not ideal, but it's my only way to climb back in.

The pinched ridges of the column give me a place to hold on as I lift my feet to the bottom. One step. Then another. With each step up, I move my hands up the pillar until the roof touches the top of my hair. I am so close now; just one more step, and then I can grab the side! One more—

*Thud.* I try to get the air back in my lungs as I lie on the ground of their porch. No! I was so close I could touch the roof. The boards groan as I lift one foot again, preparing to lift the other once I grasp the pillar with my hands again. And so the climb resumes. One step up, then another. A steady game of keeping my grasp firm and my footing secure until finally, the roof politely taps my head to inform me of my arrival. I grab the edge of the roof without wasting any time. Frantically, I try to grab anything I can with my other hand. I scramble to find something before I end up where I was a few minutes ago. The bumpiness of the layered shingles gives me nothing. One finger slips off the edge, and the rest of my hand is dangerously close to following. A hole! There is an opening! I throw my other hand to the hole's edge, swaying my body to give it enough momentum to throw my leg up. Finally! Cordelia's window is a few steps from here. One step, followed by another, I can lean over the roof's edge and scurry back through her window.

Once on solid ground again, I straighten my dress through heaving breaths. Now, where do I search?

A loud whine from a floorboard behind me shrivels my lungs in fear of what's to come. A pair of harrowed eyes staring at me stand behind me, unmoving. I can see dried blood on his hands, and I know who he is: the other child who spent the night holding his dead sister next to his wailing mother.

What do I do? Do I climb back outside? Or sprint through the children, pushing them aside along the way? If I do that, they could grab me and stop me. If I jump through the window, they could alert others by the time I safely reach the ground.

I have no choice but to make my decision in these next few moments, and my heart drops into the abyss at this prospect. Before I can think of any more possibilities to drive me further into the hole of this madness, he takes one step forward. I see a curtain of messy golden hair and piercing blue eyes staring back at me. His eyes have black markings underneath. This poor kid couldn't sleep. The air grows cold between us as the formalities have been stripped aside, leaving the stark reality bare before us. Not a word is muttered between us, and the path in front of me closes up as he steps forward, followed by his two siblings, blocking my way out. He turns back to look at his sister, snapping his neck up with such vigor I fear he may snap one of the bones. All eyes rest on me as they eagerly wait for me to state my business.

"Please," I whisper. "Please do not wake anyone else."

There is a light clamor as the siblings discuss amongst themselves, wondering what has happened for this to occur. I feel a sliver of hope reigniting inside me again. Finally, I feel as if I have taken another step toward the possibility of escape.

# Chapter Ten

## 21 January 1901

"Who are you?" The words impale me through the heart, the spike of the icicle dripping its freezing liquid into my veins. "Answer me!" Her composed stature and elegant demeanor radiates off her. Her rigid posture and cold eyes reflect her status and stare at me, waiting for me to speak. They were evidently lying in bed, but the dark purple paint stroke under their eyes indicates they were not sleeping.

The silver handle glistens in the candlelight, the damned light that drew them all to see me hiding between the shrouds of death in the child's room. A knife. I am unarmed in this battle.

"Please!" I manage to get out. I should have just left and walked off the property with Teddy. I would never be in this situation if I had. Why did I stay? Why did I come back? "I am Ann Yoder, and I am here to help!"

"Ha!" Her hand tightens on the handle as she pulls her little brother closer to her, out of the way. "What have you come here for? Hm?" She takes one step forward, and the threat of the knife breathes down my throat. "Money? Gold? Jewels?" A catch in her voice eats away at her façade as she utters the last word, "Gossip?" I can see the desperation to hide her emotion under a stoic demeanor. Her icy blue eyes match her behavior but contrast with her raven hair tied away from her face. They are shrouded in a cloak of grief; it shines from them and blinds everyone within view. Dark clouds hang above, and tears pour from them on the dead child's siblings.

"No! Nothing of the sort! I am here to help." The floorboard whines as I take a small step back, out of range from the tip of her weapon. She does not move with me. My hands clench at my sides, and I begin to wring them. What else should I say to prove myself to them? Is there anything I can say? Will any amount of convincing be enough?

"What could we possibly need your help for?"

"Your sister—"

"What about her!" She lunges forward, bringing the knife back to its original place. "What did you do? What do you know?"

"I am here to find who did this, find who…" The rest of the sentence stays in the back of my mouth, unable and unwilling to admit the truth.

"Find who killed her?" she says, with no hesitation. "The constables were already here; we have no reason to enlist help from bored civilians."

"I am no bored civilian; I work for Scotland Yard!" I plead, trying to defend the shreds of my dignity.

"A woman? Working for Scotland Yard?" Her laugh is slow before reaching a booming cackle echoing through the room. "You must truly be mad to think I would believe you! Much less accept your help!"

"It's the truth!"

"Albert." Her gaze locks with mine as she tightens her grip on her brother's arm. "Go, alert mother—"

"No!" I beg, unable to do anything more. If he leaves, the mother will call Scotland Yard. They will see me, and they will know. My shot squandered.

She takes one more step forward; the loud whine of the floorboard may be enough to wake their mother. "Tell me," she breathes. "Why should I not suspect you as my sister's killer? Why should I not carry out justice this minute?"

"Because I found something!"

"No." She shakes her head. "That is impossible. The constables found nothing aside from—" she trails off, but I know exactly what she means to say. I can see the image dancing inside her head. There is an icy chill lingering in the air as the words that remain unspoken, appearing to be suspended in the divisive ice between us.

"You know as well as I do," —the silver blade shocks my fingers as my hand brushes it gingerly to buffer the potential blow— "that they are not the pinnacle of good sleuthing." My palm curves over the knife, gently pushing it down. "You know very well why I cannot be associated with them."

"You look familiar." She examines my face in the candlelight. "I've seen you before. You were the one talking to the Chief in his carriage!"

"How could you possibly know that?"

"I know everything that happens on the property," she snaps. "Besides, your skirts got caught in the door, and you two were not quiet in your discussion. I guess it is true that you work for them, but what do you want?"

"As I have said, I want to find out who is responsible for this despicable crime."

"Why?" Her hand drops down, but her white knuckles are still tightly grasped around the knife handle. "Surely, there must be something in it for you to deem it necessary to break into our house in the middle of the night."

"I want justice," I say, brushing the selfishness of my motives away.

"I am not stupid, mistress. What will you gain?"

"A promotion." My greed lies on a stone slab between us for examination.

"Hm." She turns to face her brothers, the three of them murmur in discussion, but the sound of her voice leads them through their uncertainty. "Should we choose to help you," she begins, turning back to face me, "what do you require?"

"Just information. Answers to my questions, and I will give you privacy."

"That ship sailed quite some time ago, Miss Yoder. When you chose to illegally enter our home, to be precise." Silence ricochets off the walls and the shrapnel cuts through my lungs like a bullet. 'But what do you want to know? We will choose if we would like to answer them." She stands, unmoving in front of her brothers, as she waits for my first question. Her impeccable posture makes it appear as if she were born with a metal rod in place of a spine.

"Well." I did not expect her to agree as quickly with little more persuasion. "I suppose we could start with a simpler one before…" I trail off, not wanting to put the image of the harrowing events of the night back in their minds, but I fear in avoiding it, I have committed the crime nonetheless. I take a ragged breath before I begin hoping to stabilize my nerves. "What is your name, and how old are you?"

"Adelaide Yeats, although I suspect you already know our last name." Her foot takes one step forward, hesitating before placing it on the floorboard, dancing with her feelings. One step back toward safety or lunge toward the confrontation of reality grimly clinging to these walls is the difficult battle raging inside, one I know quite well. "I am sixteen years old." One more step forward, the shroud drapes over her with the burdensome elegance of expectation. Her rigid posture remains unwavering as she sits at the desk in her sister's chair. Not a single hair is out of place, her grief sealed away, but I can still see the waters thrashing against her fortified interior, begging to be released as the tide rises. Although, I suspect the walls are too ironclad to cause concern in her mind.

"Have you noticed anything alarming or different with Cordelia recently?"

"As I told the constables earlier," she says callously, "no. Nothing more than open windows differed in our lives."

"Please, any detail would be helpful. New dresses, new friends, disappearances, illnesses, suspicious behaviors, whispers in rooms. Anything!"

"And as I said, I would see if something was wrong! I would know, and I would fix it! The gates remain closed for a reason, no one can get in, but no one can leave either. We only have each other." Her words grow progressively louder. "I urge you to not forget yourself, Miss Yoder. You are in no place to push your boundaries."

The older of her two brothers behind her moves to stand closer and places his hand on her shoulder, as he did with his mother mere hours earlier, just a few feet away.

"Do you remember how she would run through the hallways, muddy shoes and fingers repainting the walls and floors?" he says, a slight chuckle in his voice that comes to an abrupt halt as his eyes meet the scarlet stain on the floor. The wave of nostalgia recedes as quickly as it came. The temporary bliss of the past wears off at the reminder of the brutal nature of the world.

"She was indeed rambunctious," she breathes, barely audible. Her shoulder jerks out from under her brother's hand. "My sister and I led quite different lifestyles, Miss Yoder. You have to understand there was not much for us to connect with as we've grown."

"Thank you for your honesty, Ms. Yeats." Should I ask her about the events of that night?

Would it be insensitive of me to? Would it be foolish of me not to? If I ask and upset her, I will indeed be arrested. But what if I jump from the window before the constables arrive and vanish before they find me? If I do not ask her, I risk not finding the killer and being homeless. "Can you," the words leave my tongue slowly, clinging to stay in my mouth like a paste, "describe the events of the evening, please?"

My question steals the last of my oxygen and releases the butterflies from my stomach. Their wings furiously beat against the inside of my skin, desperately trying to find their way out. What if I've crossed the line? What if I've upset her? What do I do? What do I do? What do I do?

She shifts in her chair, uncomfortable to relive the events that transpired hours before. "As I said, nothing was any different yesterday than any day before. Father left town for an important meeting in the afternoon, so it was just the four of us here. Mother spent the day making notes of chores and maintenance around the house that needed to be addressed. Albert played the day away outside yesterday, and I attended to personal matters in my room. Abraham did not arrive until dinner and left for his home soon after, as usual, when he joined us. Nothing was irregular until mother screamed, and the lanterns flying through the hallway were enough to know…" She takes a breath, and I can see her fold her hands in her lap to steady them. "To know something was wrong. I heard mother before I saw anything, and I saw Delia on the floor before I saw the blood and the light flickering from the silver handle in her chest."

She stops talking, and I cannot tell if she is done or has more to say, so I wait.

"I ran to alert the constables and grab Abraham from his home, and that was it." Her voice croaks. "I spent the evening directing the detectives and closing the gates to deter people because I couldn't go back… I couldn't see her again, not like that. I could not subject myself to that again…" She trails off, and a single tear rests on her face, but she rapidly wipes it away.

Unsure of what to do next, I let the silence eat away at the peaceful unrest of the room. Should I ask more questions? Should I ask someone else?

"If these answers are to your satisfaction, Miss Yoder, my brothers may have more they would like to add," she says, looking up at her brother. He stands next to her, Abraham, I presume, staring bleakly at the area in front of him. His rumpled suit reflects his emotions. His blonde hair is tousled, and it is evident he could barely pull himself together enough to drag himself out of bed.

"Right." He sighs, "I suppose you'll have the same questions for me." His words are slow and deep. "I am Abraham Yeats, and I am eighteen years old. I cannot attest to suspicious behavior, as last night was the first time I've seen Delia in a few weeks." The water rises in his eyes, spilling on his face at the recollection of his sister. "I should've visited more. I planned on visiting more…"

"You did what you needed to do, Abe," a quiet voice squeaks. These are the first words I hear from the younger sibling.

Abraham's head drops. "But I should've been here! I would've been able to do something! If—"

"If you were here, you would have been as powerless as the rest of us, or dead as well, Abraham," Adelaide interrupts.

Her older brother's hand blanches as Addie grabs his wrists and tightens her grip, supporting him and keeping him upright when he cannot. However, when I look closer, I can see his hand mimics hers, and his facial expression mirrors hers as well. Underneath her stony stoic façade is a crumbling wall frantically attempting to rebuild itself before anyone notices. Tears run down his face, and Adelaide wipes them away, soothing him. She is trying to stitch together the gaping hole torn in the fabric of their lives, but her expected acts of servitude go unnoticed.

"The last time I saw her, she was upset because I was in her room while I was looking for her." He chuckles before continuing. "I guess she became secretive about her room when I left because she was never like that."

"That is a trait she acquired not too long ago," Adelaide remarks.

"I just miss her," he begins again. "I missed her even before last night. Delia loved messing with all of us. We all expected that to fade as she grew, but she remained young at heart, and now I suppose that is the case. She will stay forever young. Forever a child." He pauses to catch his breath. A flicker of a faint smile lights up his face as he recounts these memories. However, his face darkens, and his shoulders tense as I realize he will carry on his narrative toward the dreaded end. "The blood was… everywhere. We all knew the impossibility of her survival. Mother, Albert, and I sat with her." His head jerks up from the stain to glare at his sister. "Adelaide, why didn't you? How could you leave little Delia on the floor like that?"

"Abraham!" she cries out in disbelief. "Someone had to step up and take care of the responsibilities since the acting head of household," she juts her head forward at him, "could not. Duties do not magically stop when bad things happen, although I don't suspect you know much about that."

"And just what is that supposed to mean?!" He explodes in a rage; his blazing eyes are bloodthirsty and seeking vengeance. I am unsure how to proceed, but I know they will need to calm down before I can do anything else. "She is our sister, Addie. You should have stopped to show it." His words slow down, and I can see his anger subsiding. "She was our sister, and now…"

"And now she is being taken care of as she should be in her condition! Now she will be properly buried, so we can visit. Now the family can grieve in peace without being burdened by these responsibilities. Just because my efforts differ from yours does not make them any less credible!"

He pauses, takes a deep breath, and looks at her, "You are right, Addie."

"I am not as heartless as you all make me out to be! I have duties and obligations to attend to in your stead because we stand to lose everything if I don't; I stand to lose everything. Mother and Father have each other and all their current assets. You and Albert have that wealth after them, but I will have nothing without a husband. I am the only one who grasps the full severity of these situations because I am the only one blinded by the pitfalls of the future. So do not judge me too harshly, brother, as I am only doing what I must to survive." The sincerity of her voice makes me inclined to believe her. She is telling the truth.

The now youngest child steps forward in the room, standing between his siblings, Adelaide sitting behind him while Abraham stands, resting his hand on his younger brother's shoulder. In this pose, the three of them complete a grim portrait, but it will always be missing the piece of little Delia. The youngest one is an identical, miniaturized version of his older brother. Time does not make his eyes any easier to look at. They appear to be caved into his skull, severely sunken in, and blackened from lack of sleep.

"I would like to start now," he squeaks.

"Darling, are you sure you are up for this?" Adelaide croons.

He responds with a solemn nod. I take this as an invitation to continue. The three of them stand with their arms entwined, but a shadow still rests over their faces.

"I will begin with the same questions as I did for your siblings," I say softly, hesitating to cross any unwarranted borders or cause undue stress, especially to a child. "Your name and age?"

"I am Albert, and I am thirteen." His voice is barely audible.

"And can you think of anything out of the ordinary recently involving your sister?" He shifts his eyes around the room before shaking his head, refusing to look me in the eye. "Albert," I say, moving to see his face, "I can only help if you are honest with me. Are you positive there is not anything you believe to be strange?"

He is defeated, and I can see the wheels in his head turning as he contemplates his answer. "I have a secret about Delia, but Mother and Father cannot know." He looks at me with urgency in his eyes.

"Albert, what is this about?" Adelaide queries, her voice frantic.

"Albert, why didn't you say anything before?" Abraham interjects.

"How was he supposed to tell you while you were gallivanting in a different part of the city, Abraham? This is not a topic you need to concern yourself with, as you haven't been concerned with other familial matters lately," she snaps. Abraham remains silent. "Albert, what do you know!"

"I would see Delia sneaking away at night sometimes." He shifts, twisting his hands and shuffling his legs. "She would never tell me where she was going, but she would be back in the morning before anyone would notice."

"Why did you never say anything?" Adelaide explodes, seething as her hands clench at her sides.

He is silent like his brother for a few minutes as he contemplates his answer. "I do not even know if she ever left the yard! I do not know where she went, but I only knew because I would check on her at night."

"Why would you check—" I start before being interrupted by Adelaide.

"You know Mother's rules, and you did nothing? No one is allowed out after dark. No one is to step past the gates."

"I did not think it was important! It is a stupid rule anyway!"

"Well, look where we are now, burying our baby sister because she thought the same thing."

"Addie!" Abraham protests. "He could not have known! None of us knew what would happen! You are blaming the wrong person while the murderer runs free."

"I would give anything to go back in time and say something. I wish I would have stopped her or told you sooner, but I—" A tear trickles down Albert's cheek, and after a moment, he buries his head in his hands.

"It is not your fault," Abraham says. "We cannot know if anything you said or did would change what happened."

Adelaide continues clenching her fists as her nostrils flare, as she watches her brothers.

"You said you would check on your sister at night sometimes. Why?" I ask, taking advantage of the silence before another explosion happens.

Albert looks at Adelaide from the corner of his eye and shuffles toward his brother before speaking. "I would hear voices from her room."

"Voices?" I query, nervous that Adelaide will get upset again, but she remains silent. "Can you think of anything said? Or possibly even describe the sound of it?"

I sit with bated breath as I wait for him to respond, hoping to give me anything to identify this person. Hundreds of people will board the ship in a few hours; one characteristic would help narrow them down. I cannot let the murderer escape.

"I often dismissed these sounds as the wind or Delia talking to herself. It was always dark, so I never saw anyone else through the keyhole. I'm afraid I could not pick out anything in particular." He stares at the wall and does not break his gaze. "But now that I think about it… the voice was a bit forceful. It would sound as if the wind howled through her window."

"Did you hear these voices earlier tonight? Before—" I trail off, unsure if I should finish the sentence. By the end, my voice is nearly a whisper as a tear rolls down his cheek. A single, slow nod is his response.

"Yes," he mumbles, discreetly flicking his tears away.

"Did you see someone in her room? Did you touch anything?" My heart breaks as his face contorts as the memories resurface in his brain.

The tears begin to fall more liberally, and he no longer tries to wipe them away. I can see him wrestling with his thoughts and the images forever seared into his mind. I gently place my hand on his shoulder to help comfort him before he answers.

"She was the only one in the room. All I could see was her lying on the floor… and the blood. There was so much blood." He pauses, ducking his head like a turtle retreating into its shell to avoid the ugly confrontation of the night. "I ran to Mother's room right after. I was too afraid to see her face, but I cannot seem to see anything else now."

As Adelaide turns and wipes away the tears from his cheeks, Abraham embraces him, no longer angry.

"I believe we have given you more than enough information, Miss Yoder," Adelaide announces, turning back to me.

I take this as a signal it is time for me to leave and take one step toward the door.

"But," she continues, "you have not given us any yet."

"I'm sorry?"

"You said you came across clues and information the other constables missed. Please, enlighten us on what you've found."

I suppose it is their right to know, although I suspect they will not take kindly to it. I shuffle back to the bed, where I was standing before, bend down and grab the suitcase handle. Once it is lifted on the bed, I turn the clasps, revealing everything inside. The shoes, dresses, and ticket.

Adelaide's hand covers her mouth. "What is this?" she demands, although I know she already knows. "America" is written in bolded letters across the top. There are few other possibilities.

"I think you know," I whisper, hoping the slight tremor in my voice is masked.

Adelaide's face contorts from this shocking remark; she is caught off guard. "I am appalled at your assumptions. Cordelia had no friends outside these walls. I may not have known my sister very well, but I know her well enough to know she would not deliberately leave us. She was too young to know and to even think of this. I believe you have your facts wrong."

Adelaide shakes her head in disbelief. "What would she have done… How could she even think of doing this? How could she not tell anyone? How… how…"

Cordelia wanted to live and see how the world was outside of the distorted images she brought from the entirety of her life confined to these grounds. After all, it is impossible to properly fix the wounds of the past if it is sewn up while infection ravages within. But she knew the answers to all these questions.

As she trails off, she is overcome with hysterics. Her breathing comes in shallow gasps, and it sounds like she is trying to swallow any trace amount of air to keep herself alive. Her face reddens, and I can see her hands balled into fists at her side. I am unaware of what to do or how to console her.

"You cannot blame yourself…"

Adelaide interrupts in a fit of rage, "I do not! Her decision would have cost us everything, her everything, and all of her volition! We would have had to have carried on without her! Did she really expect no one to notice? Her choice would have fallen on everyone but her. She would get freedom while the rest of us cleaned up her mess. Her reputation, our reputation, would be destroyed. The family line would end with us."

I stare at her in shock. Her quick dismissal of her sister is astounding.

"Adelaide!" Abraham yells. "She was a child and felt the need to leave! That is more telling than anything else right now! She was willing to give up everything to pursue a life that was not here. She was just a girl, and we would have lost her either way. Think of that!"

After a moment, Adelaide stops her episode abruptly, wipes away a few stray tears, and her face reverts to its normal color. "I am sorry for my outburst. I was just taken by surprise; it will not happen again. Please forgive me."

A switch flips in her demeanor; as I stare at her smoothing wrinkles out on her dress coolly, I find it hard to fathom her eruption just moments earlier. I am perplexed at the rapidity in which she switched emotions.

"Who are you, and what are you doing in my house!" a voice snaps.

A white, billowy cloud of silk and cotton appears behind the children, and the large red stain on the lower half is only display as an exhibit of the failures of the world. The mother. She seems stiff as a board, and it is evident she did not sleep either.

"I am here to help solve this case," I say calmly, hoping she will listen to reason. "My name is—"

"We have constables doing that for us! The services of a stranger are not needed!" She whips around to her children. "Why are you willingly enabling the imagination of outsiders?"

"Addie and I—"

"It's Adelaide," the mother interrupts. "Your sister is no longer a child, and you must stop addressing her as such," she snaps.

"Mother, Cordelia is dead." Abraham's voice cracks, and he pauses. It is difficult for him to admit this. His bloodshot eyes tear up as he continues. "Adelia will never grow up, so forgive me for not caring about such minor frivolities!" He says, as his siblings say nothing to avoid her sharp words.

"Just like the people loitering outside of our gates all evening?"

"She already found more than the constables did all night," Adelaide pipes up.

"What?" Alexandra gasps incredulously.

"She has done more to help than the detectives!"

"What did you find?" she demands.

I look at Adelaide, hoping she will tell her mother as I am unsure if it is my place to say. This news might be better received coming from family.

"She found a suitcase… full of Cordelia's clothes and a ticket to America," Adelaide blurts.

I move to the side so Alexandra can see the last plans her daughter made spread over her bed. Before their mother can react, Adelaide takes Albert by the shoulders and ushers him to his room. As she steps out, she whispers to him, "It is past your bedtime. We can discuss this in the morning, but you should go to sleep." She then turns to Abraham and tells him the same.

Before stepping into the hallway, he cries, "You know why I had to leave, why I couldn't stay—"

"Yes, Abraham. I know," she reassures him patiently. "I'm sorry for not remembering that earlier. You did what you had to do, and that's that," she says, walking out of the room with him.

"No. I refuse this to be true," she chokes once the room is empty. "I know my Cordelia, and I know she would never run away… surely you are mistaken. The killer must've packed this suitcase… not my baby…" Her shoulders heave as she begins to cry deeply. "This is impossible. Cordelia never wanted to run away. She would have…" Alexandra stops, trying to fight back the tears. "She would have told me if she was unhappy."

She resumes her wailing once again. The sound starts low, but her crying becomes guttural, and I feel like I have been punched in the stomach. I debate responding, but I know the impact inspiring false hope can have. Blood would have been present on the dresses. There is no other logical explanation.

"Do you have any children?" she heaves between sobs.

"No," the single word echoes through the room.

"The world is a cruel place. Little ones have no reason to see the horrors beyond them. My children needed no companionship aside from each other. You know I am right. You know what the world is like. Deep down, you can see this was the right choice. The world would have eaten them alive, and they would not be kids anymore. We would have hollow shells instead of people. It is a terrible thing to lose a child in your own lifetime, it should never happen to anyone, yet it happened in our own home last night, and now our family no longer feels safe in our own home from strangers who think they are privy to this grief by barging through our doors."

The swirls of darker wood on the floor are mesmerizing. The one next to the nail sticking out of the floorboards is quite large. I cannot remove my eyes from the boards in fear of seeing Alexandra's anger.

"I believe it would be best if you left now," she advises slowly, and I comply.

As I drag my feet out of the room and through the hallway, I look out the windows above the front door. The sky is streaked with dark purple and playful pink as the sun begins to rise. The gates at Scotland Yard would be closed and locked. Is this the beginning of the rest of my life? Fleeing from one scene only to find there is nowhere to go? I continue this drudge to the front door, but before my hand rests on the front doorknob, a voice echoes in the open stairway.

"Miss Yoder..." I look at Adelaide, waiting for her to finish. "Here." She shoves a piece of parchment into my hand. "It's a drawing I made of Delia. If you can use it to find someone who recognizes her... Please find who did this."

I glance down at the parchment. Playful lines are etched across it, and through this picture, I can see an entirely different life on the paper than I saw before me on the floor a few hours before. The floorboards shake underfoot as a *thud, thud, thud-thud-thud* sound grows louder, followed by a child's giggle. The light in the hallway miraculously transforms into a golden haze, radiating to everyone within the stretch as the thudding gets closer. The culprit of the noise becomes evident as she runs around the curve. An infectious laugh bounces between my ears as her contagious smile lights the house up. It only takes seconds for me to recognize that this is how Cordelia must have appeared to her family.

She reaches her hand out for me to take, beckoning me to join her band of mischief in this house.

"Come home," she says.

As quickly as she ran toward me, she runs away, taking the light with her before I could give her an answer.

I cannot think of anything to say as the knife of remorse digs further into my stomach.

Ah, and so the mystery of the occupant of the room next door is solved. I look into her eyes and faintly see the same expression as in her family members. I have been wrong about Adelaide. She has not limited her mourning entirely, just in the public eye. Behind her steely, impenetrable gaze, there is a small crack. I nod to her before replying, "Of course, Adelaide. I am sorry for your loss once again." Beneath her stoic demeanor is a grieving child, unable to show her pain.

"I must apologize for my family once again. You will have to excuse them."

Before I can object, she brushes her hand across her face and disappears up the stairs. I stand alone and cannot help transporting back to when I first arrived just a few hours prior. Although the pain and darkness that lingered in the atmosphere have dissipated slightly, the wails still echo through the walls, and the hole in the heart widens. Despite the terrible night having passed, this house will remain forever changed. There will be some element, some piece, always aching to be complete.

Adelaide stops at the top of the stairs, and her composure has returned, overlooking me and everything else on the entryway floor, waiting to watch me leave. Before any of her other family members join her, she looks as if she could be the mistress of the house. The elegance of her presence is striking, and her maturity and readiness to accept the cruelty of society is admirable.

# Chapter Eleven

## 22 January 1901

It takes more strength to open the gates than it did to close them behind Teddy not too long ago, yet I hesitate before walking through them. In leaving, I willingly give up on a piece of this case and my direct connection to this family.

My cold, clammy hands cool the iron bars resting between my convulsing palms, as if they are aware of the stakes and risks of what is all but guaranteed to happen by the night's end. But too much needs to be done; I cannot afford to lose more time to Hesitation's dawdling mind. I devise a solution and clasp my fingers together. My bones crush each other under my grasp, but the tremors lessen significantly. Hoping the combined strength will be enough to make it appear as though the shaking has stopped.

Alexandra's last words echo through my head. I cannot shake the anger, betrayal, and disappointment she exuded. I was helping. I was just trying to help. Dusk lingers just out of grasp. Another day has faded out of view, and I am still far from reaching solid ground. I remain tired, but no amount of sleep will solve the problem, so I suppose there is no reason to go to bed if this cycle continues. Besides, I have more pressing matters to tend to.

"Darling." Teddy's voice is enough to bring me back to the present, back to the street corner we agreed to meet at. "How did it go?"

I say nothing. Not sure which words to use. The blood in my veins comes to a screeching halt yet again. Bells and whistles rage in my head, causing my face to flush from the pent-up steam under my skin. My mind floods with urgent reminders of how far behind I am in this case.

"Based on your vacant expression, I assume you did not have much luck since we last spoke," he drawls. Every second between each spaced-out word bludgeons my lungs.

Again, not a sound leaves my mouth. My hands clasp again, and my iron grip as I hold them causes my bones to ache under the crushing pressure. I am positive my fingers will be forever changed and dis-figured now.

"Need I remind you of how far behind you already are? Ann, if you wish to solve this case, you need to find more evidence soon. What are you going to do? How do you expect to find the killer with no clues? No suspects?"

He is right. I twist my fingers in their iron grip, feeling as if the bones inside have begun turning to powder from the grinding. "I... I do not know Teddy. There are not any more leads for me to pursue. I have reached a dead end. Perhaps this is it. What if this case will remain forever unsolved?" As I utter these words, a piece of my soul shatters. My lungs stop, and my feelings from the Yeats house reprieve. An icy liquid pumps through my heart and spreads through my veins. A sliver of me will always carry this sickening feeling, poisoning me.

"Nonsense! There is no time to waste. We must get started immediately then, my dear," he says. "Surely, there must be some clue somewhere."

The sticky liquor of dread fills me as a weight drops on my shoulders at the reminder of this suffocating time constraint. The monstrous murderer of a young girl is roaming through the streets, waiting to strike again, free to live without the consequences.

"You do realize no one else can help, right? That it is just the two of us! Time is quite literally of the essence, darling."

Once again, he is right. He is truly the only person who helps me look after myself. Samuel would've helped. He'd have the answer and given all his time to show me where to find it. Before he decided to burn that bridge.

I can't shake this nagging feeling that I drove him to sever our friendship. Was it my fault? Could I have done something differently?

"Where shall we go, dear?" Teddy's voice is enough to remind me of my problems right now.

"I-I don't know," I manage to mutter. "A store? A restaurant? Any building, I guess." But what is the point? What are the odds anyone will have anything new to offer to this mystery?

"All right, then." He holds out his hand for me to take. "Let's get started then."

I glance at his palm, then up at him. "What will they say?"

He wiggles his fingers, showing his ringless hand. "They will not know we are unwed."

The canopies above me belong to the storefronts of the business I pass by, protecting me from being blinded by the sun's rays. Only certain ones chose to decorate their exterior with these wilting flowers, while others left it bare. As I look out before me, I am surrounded by a continuous line of red brick that has been painted brown with the dust and grime that rests atop the city. The windows appear to be the only distraction from this. Their strategic placing makes them line up precisely the same way in rows and columns. Under each window is a strip of stained white brick decorated with the same shade of brown as the surrounding bricks. These windows are also adorned with bars extending out before pointing up, allowing room for a small planter to fit.

The winds change, harboring a gust with enough vigor to sweep an adult off their feet, pulling me out from the safety of the sidewalk and closer to the buildings. I keep an iron fist around Adelaide's drawings, and the sides flutter up, sifting through the wind. Perhaps I will finally find the answers I am in dire need of. I am running out of time, and even a single clue would be helpful.

"What do you have in your hand?"

Teddy's voice shatters this silence, causing the clamor of the streets to come crashing down around me. Each sound is clear and distinctive, leaving little room for quietness.

"You startled me." I turn to face him before continuing. "This." The parchment unrolls, revealing the ink tattooing itself with the face of Cordelia. "This is a picture Adelaide drew of Delia. Perhaps if others recognize her face, they may come forward with any information." A smile creeps across my face as a flicker of hope begins to gleam.

"Why is her portrait important? It is pointless to remind them of the image of a dead child," he says coldly.

His frigid words snuff the kindling ember, leaving nothing more than wisps of smoke as proof of its existence.

"Perhaps it may be futile, but it is better than standing idly by for my imminent termination," I rebut. "Besides, these children seldom left the grounds of their home. If someone happened to see her, I doubt her parents would have known of her excursion. They could've seen her with the murderer."

His eyes move calmly and collectively as he ponders this. "I suppose this may not be entirely useless," he utters. "It is better than doing nothing."

"Let's go, dear. You can help me ask people."

His hand wraps around mine, pulling me into his web, gluing me to the strands perched between the towering branches of a tree. Together, we cross the street, walking further away from the Yeats' house, further away from the sanctuary of grief.

"Where shall we start, darling?"

"I suppose at the first establishment we come across," I say, thankful to have him with me. Surely, we should find a piece of the puzzle between the two of us. But what if we are unsuccessful? What if this quest plants us in front of yet another brick wall? What will I do then?

Towering buildings sway before us, parting to grant us access to the heart of the city. The formidable giants offer an assortment of goods for passersby to ogle on their commutes. The sun reflects from an unending line of windows around us, blinding us with the realization of the task ahead of us. This would take all day. There is no better time to start than now. A few paces from us, the black door of a store beckons us inside, calling us to inquire with the shop owner.

The door swivels inward, granting us passage into the sanctuary of lost gadgets and invaluable heirlooms that found an asylum for a desperately low cost. These treasures lie in wait for the transfer to an unknown spot until the day comes for them to return here once again.

"Welcome…" a voice says. "Step into my shop of trinkets and baubles. Would you care for a ring, mistress?" His eyebrows perk up at the prospect of making a sale, trying desperately to rehome even just one measly trinket in his collection, possibly the only deal for quite some time.

"No, sir," I say. "We are only here to ask you a few questions if you do not mind."

I unroll the drawing, and a glimmer of recognition lights his eyes. He knows her.

"Have you seen this young woman?" I demand.

He turns to Teddy before answering. "Why?" he demands. "Are her parents looking for her?"

"No," Teddy begins. "They—"

"They are looking for her murderer," I interrupt, unwilling to be complicit in his ignorance of my presence.

His eyes widen in disbelief. "No," he mutters. "No… this cannot be." He stares at us, hoping for some telltale sign of a fictitious story. "She was here only a few days ago. She was only a child."

"Tell me," I begin, knowing answers are lurking between the shadows of miscellaneous items scattered throughout the shop. "How do you know her?"

His eyes no longer search our faces. Instead, they inspect the dust inhabiting the cracks between the crevices of the floorboard planks. "She came in here asking for help finding a trunk she could pack her clothes in."

Could this be where she purchased the suitcase I found under her bed? Her plans to leave must have been recent, or she certainly would've tried to wrangle one from a more prestigious source.

"She was so excited…" He pauses before continuing. "Her attitude was quite infectious." A smile creeps upon his face as this memory resurfaces.

"Was anyone else with her? Waiting outside or shopping with her?" I cannot contain my eagerness at the prospect of a new clue.

He stops, gingerly stroking his chin as his eyes flash back to the day in question, searching for any inkling of recognition. "No," he firmly replies. "There was no one else in the store with her, but she was quite eager to leave. There may have been someone waiting for her outside."

"Did—"

"Unfortunately, I did not see what this person looked like." He answers my question before I finish asking. His pitiful eyes bore into the wooden floorboards in the hopes of evading my hopeful eyes. "I do, however," he continues, "know she left after she was unsuccessful in finding what she was looking for. I am not sure where she flew away to, but she was desperate to leave."

My gaze shifts to Teddy, uncertain of what to do next. My hope remains shattered on the ground, too fragmented to even bother trying to pick up.

"I do not believe there is anything else we can learn here, dear," he whispers. "Perhaps we should try our luck elsewhere."

What am I supposed to do now? This cannot be all I am meant to find here. Surely there must be something else—something to help me solve this case, or I am doomed. Anything. A cold, clammy hand touches my forehead as I attempt to cool the heat that rushes to my face. I turn to face the door, trying to grasp the situation at hand as calmly as I can.

Accepting defeat, I begrudgingly thank the shopkeeper for his answer and take a step out of the door, struggling to let go of the tattered tether of faith grounding me to this store. Without it, I am floating in limbo, unsure of where to go and powerless to control my next steps. Watery sludge holds me in this state, slowly crawling against every inch of my body.

"Where shall we go next, dear?" His once sweet voice sounds like nails raking across a classroom chalkboard.

"I… I don't…" My words struggle to fight their way up my throat. All of my organs smash together into one suffocating blob in my chest, indecipherable from each other.

"Home?" he tries.

"No." My head shakes so vigorously that I fear it will fall from my shoulders. "No, you know that if anyone sees me, I could be arrested for trespassing. I cannot…" My words trail off, leading into the frightening abyss of destitution that awaits me if I do not find the killer. Tonight is my last night there if I am not successful. How do I wish to spend this last night? Admitting defeat and granting myself one last night of rest before I am forced on the streets? Or persisting with a wavering flicker of hope to bring justice to their family?

"Darling, people are staring. We must start moving. Where shall we go?"

"There is nowhere to go," I mutter. "We have exhausted every resource to no avail. There is nothing else we can search for. If we question the other shop owners, we forfeit our remaining time that could be better spent searching elsewhere."

"We need to get married."

A dry laugh escapes from my mouth. "Are you mad?"

"It is lunacy we have not done so already; we should have wed ages ago. It is your last chance—"

"My last chance at what?" The words slither off my tongue, ready to bite anyone within range of their venomous fangs. "My last chance to give up what little individuality I have left? My last chance to be yet another woman trapped in the legal confines of marriage?"

"Do not be ridiculous," he rasps. "I am afraid you do not have many choices. You can let the others ravage and pillage through what's left of your reputation, but whatever is remaining, they will destroy. There is no more time to keep waiting."

"Once word about this gets out, I will be ruined, dragging you down with me. Why are you offering to help?" This is not his problem; he can flee from this situation, free from any blame or scrutiny.

"I must be quite honest with you, Ann. I'm in love with you. Since I first showed up at your door, I cannot get you off my mind. I never want to leave the source, the home, for all these feelings keeping me alive, driving every breath and beat of my heart."

"Where will we live? Why can I not stay with—"

"Darling." His hand squeezes my shoulder, and I know what he will say before he does. "Should anyone find out, we will be in this same position again. My cousin will only take us in once we are married."

My mind clings to the last bit of rationality remaining, but he is right. I cannot keep my focus on the Yeats when my own life is ripping apart at the seams. With this marriage, I would have a roof over my head and security. If I chose to stay with him outside of such a contract, there would be nothing left of my reputation should someone likely find out. The few remaining job prospects would disappear, and my only hope would be to run away, yet I would be stranded here without the money to make that happen. I still feel deep mourning as I prepare to sever my old life with my own hand. I turn around, ready to face a new life ahead. I have no other option but to accept this and continue. No good will come from dwelling on what might have happened.

I look down at the drawing in my hand, hoping there is some clue written between the lines to reveal the identity of the killer. But that's not how it works. The pencil marks animate, her loose curls fall from her shoulders as she shakes her head once in warning.

The wind snatches the paper before I can rub my eyes and look again. Did the drawing move? Logically, I know that is impossible, but I know what I saw.

Despite whatever happened, I know I have no choice but to do what I must. With or without her approval, I have to do this to survive.

My heart breaks, and my lungs ache as I utter the words of defeat that will sign my fate away, "Let's get married." And so it is decided.

# Chapter Twelve

## 22 January 1901

The chapel is empty, save for the Priest, who looks disapprovingly at us as we enter. The dingy, gray interior seems no different than the inside of the holding cells at Scotland Yard, except for the three stained glass murals on all of the walls aside from the one containing the door. The fractured, colorful glass brings more light than all the feeble flames from the candles combined, but it still offers very little. Each flicker gives a glimpse of a new species of vermin running freely, scavenging for crumbs amidst the large flakes of dirt on the stone floors. Tattered pews line the ground, all facing the central mural, drawing attention to the image of the biblical tale etched from various fragments of painted shards.

I have always believed it to be beautiful to see how something that has been shattered beyond repair could be salvaged in such a way to make something of the other damaged pieces. I suppose this is what it means to be human; constantly shattering only to have these broken pieces worked into a tapestry as a testament to our lives, with the grief and happiness discreetly woven between the cracks. Perhaps this fragment of life will be incorporated into my stained glass story. The shambles of my career and freedom may bring some light and beauty to the story of my life when viewed collectively.

"Excuse us, sir, but we are looking to get married," Teddy says as the large oak door slams behind him with a loud, dull thud.

The sound echoes between the four walls, holding no one but the two of us and the priest. He stares at us as the thudding continues reverberating through our bones, even as the echo has subsided.

He glowers, pondering his next move before he responds. "And just why, pray tell, do you wish to do so?"

My heart stops, and the dust lays suspended in the air as the answer waits to be spoken. What if he does not approve? What will we do then? All of the other churches will likely have the same reaction should this question, when, this question comes up again. What should I say? What—

"Because I should like the two of us to be married." The words rush out before I can give it another thought. "Legitimized in the eyes of God, our souls bound for eternity."

The priest's eyes shift between us, scanning us for a reason to object. "When does the happy couple wish to undergo such a ceremony?"

My hand slips back into Teddy's, knowing time is not on our side. "We were hoping quite soon actu—"

"Now," he interrupts, unable to wait any longer. "We would like to wed today if possible, Father."

"What an unusual request," he drawls, thinking over every word before spitting them out. "Although… this is not the first time such an appeal has been made."

Teddy's grip loosens as he breathes a sigh of relief. "Thank—"

"I did not say I would do this," the priest interrupts. "Hiding something unseemly, are we?" he rasps. "Unsavory, perhaps?"

"How dare you imply—" I begin, letting the heat of my anger boil the words frothing from my mouth.

"Darling." Teddy's eyes dart, signaling me to follow his lead. "There is no use covering this anymore. You are correct, Father. We are trying to hide this union."

The priest's eyes gleam at this confirmation of his correctness. "I am no fool, you know." And I want nothing more than to rid his face of that smug smile.

"We wish to get married without the influence of her family, Father. We want to marry for love and nothing more," he continues lying.

"And it would be unseemly to think there are any ulterior reasons, Father," I say, unable to let go of the hostility he greeted us with. But, if Teddy is not careful where he treads, we could still be turned away.

"I suppose," the priest breathes. "That is a reason our Lord would approve of." His mumbles and grumbles echo through the hall, ricocheting off the stone wall before the words of his final verdict shoot us directly. "For a fee."

"For a fee?!" I blurt out, unable to contain my surprise.

"Father, surely there must be another way—"

"I am sorry, dear boy, but that is the only way I will ordain this marriage."

"How much?" I ask. "How much must we pay?"

"Well, how much is your commitment to each other worth?" He raises his eyebrows, hoping to get the most out of this deal.

What a conniving old man. "Father, I do not think we can put a price on our relationship." I turn to Teddy, and I know this much is true. He has been by my side for as long as I can remember. Would I calculate the worth based on how long we have been together? Or from the physical cost of the damages and consequent repairs? Any way I look at this, it is impossible to separate myself from our relationship, and any way I calculate our worth, I realize the cost to fix my problem will be far too high for us to afford. Perhaps we are already married in every way that counts.

"Teddy, I am not sure about this." I pull him aside to shield us from the disparaging looks of the priest.

"I am not sure what other choice we have, darling."

"Maybe we could search for another priest; surely someone else could help us."

"I would not be so sure of that," he interrupts. "Marriage in such haste will not be approved by many. And even then, there will still be a fee, I assure you. For our safety and for yours."

"Safety?" I laugh.

"And discretion," he whispers. "If you ask one too many priests this request, they may get… ideas."

Of course. I should've known. In trying to avoid one monster of defeat, I have encountered the same one in a different mask.

"Teddy," I pause, thinking of all his possible reactions before finishing, not wanting to choose the wrong word to make more of a scene. "Are you sure about this? Are we rushing into this?"

"Darling, it's now or never. It's this or nothing."

"Teddy, what if I just live with you without us being married?" He's right. I will be on the streets by the end of the night if I cannot find another plan, another way to survive each day.

"You would be living in sin, my dear," the priest hisses. "Sin."

"No, Ann." Spittle flies before hitting the ground. "I cannot keep discussing this with you! I want to do this because I love you. We have been friends from our youth, together up 'til now, and now together for eternity. We have been married in every way that matters; now, we are just putting our relationship in writing. Nothing more." As the words soften at the end, my lungs close up as my heart skips a beat. We are doing this. We are having a wedding, and not entirely out of necessity.

"Father, we agree to your terms. We would like you to marry us."

"Yes, Father." The echo barely reaches my ears. "The sooner, the better."

"Hm," he grumbles. "And the fee?"

"Teddy, I don't have anything… maybe I can find something in the basement of Scotland Yard…"

"No, dear." The words slice through my sentence. "That won't be necessary. Father, I have an old pocket watch, I assure you, is quite valuable."

"Teddy, I have never seen you with—"

"I keep it hidden—"

"Don't you interrupt me again! Let me finish what I have to say." He recoils from this sharp command.

The silence is full of all the words that creep out from the crevices, wanting to be spoken but waiting for someone to pluck up the courage to free them.

"I would like to see this pocket watch." The priest is the first brave soul to shatter the silence.

Teddy pulls from his vest a gold-plated pocket watch encrusted with emeralds as green as the rolling fields of Ireland. The gold chain dangles in the air as he unclasps it from his vest, handing it to the priest, allowing me to see the design engraved on its face. A tree grows on the gold plate, with leaves hanging on the wild and loose branches clinging to their source of life. Two lone limbs from the lower boughs curve into the open area between the tree and the ground. The mangled branches twist into the letters "AY" on either side of the tree trunk. They litter the roots with their decaying bodies, except one, fluttering gently in the wind on its way to join the others.

"AY?" I puzzle, trying to decipher what the initials stand for.

"The engraver put my initials in the wrong order."

"Why didn't you get it corrected?"

"Why bother? The important information is there. And besides, I could not afford a replacement."

"This will do quite nicely. I accept your offer and can wed you at once. Are there any preparations you shall need to make? Any family members you would like to join?" His forehead wrinkles from his eyebrow, arching in a sly, cocky manner, knowing our response.

"Father, we have other plans this evening and would like to hurry this along." I squeeze Teddy's hand, urging him to be cautious with his blunt requests in fear of causing the priest to change his mind.

"Of course, we must make haste for the happy couple," he drawls. "And the rings?"

Teddy pulls two simple golden bands from his pocket.

"Where did you get those?" I ask.

"I struck up a deal with a certain shop owner, one I believe you know." He grins.

Air bellows through the stone walls. The loud wail creates such a ruckus as though a wailing widow stands in the room expressing the grief of her late beloved husband. The three of us stare at each other, afraid to interrupt her tale of loss.

"Today we are gathered," the priest begins once the widow's deep breaths have ceased, and the iron chandeliers have slowed and let their flames flicker again, "to celebrate the matrimony of you two. From this moment on, your souls will be bound, entwined, and meshed together."

Permanently. The word runs through my mind before I can stop it.

"From here on out, you shall be seen as but one body, as one person by others, and by our holy God. With these rings, your fates are now sealed for eternity. If anyone has any reason to object to this wedding, speak now or forever hold your peace..."

Silence echoes through my ears as I contemplate saying something in hopes it will calm my heart and my nerves. The priest looks between Teddy and me, waiting for one of us to show some signal, some indication of our hesitancy to this binding ritual. But we have no choice. We have existed together for ages, we are just now putting on a label, or a ring, I suppose, for others to know of and see our relationship without the secrecy and further pain resulting from it being released. A single head nod is enough for the priest to continue.

"With these rings," he shoves a gold band on my finger and turns to cram the other on Teddy's, "and your signatures on the document below." My hand jerks from the white feather as it is forced between my fingers. A drop of black ink spills on the parchment. A single blob now stains this legally binding document, smearing as I try to brush the problem aside.

"The ink will dry out soon, darling. We do not have all day," Teddy hisses under his breath.

He is right. Ann Yoder. I can see my name clearly for the last time, for it will never be the same again. Teddy's name appears next to mine, as it has been on all our drawings and stories for years, but this time, a little piece of my soul leaves my body with every letter he prints. Although, I suspect this is nothing more than wedding jitters, nothing more than nerves over the death sentence I face if we cannot solve this problem.

"I now pronounce you man and wife."

It is done. The rest of the words fade into the distance, and the hopeful gleam in Teddy's eyes is enough to make my heart race faster. There is no going back now. I suppose I could destroy this flimsy piece of paper, but I'll always know, the priest will know, and once we walk through this door, others will know, too.

"What now?" I ask, turning away from the priest to look at Teddy and only Teddy.

"Well, wife…" A small laugh escapes my mouth at the sight of his goofy grin. "We should get the remainder of your belongings and finally settle in a home."

Home. I suppose that is the next logical step.

"But what home?" I blurt.

"Now that we are married, we have a house we can go to. We have a home for a while."

But what about the Yeats? What about the murderer running rampant in the streets? Who will comfort them? Who will help them?

"Darling." The grin plastered on his face is infectious. "Would you mind stopping by the Yeats' house with me on the way?"

The corners of his mouth drop. "Again? After how you left last time? Do you wish to upset them even more? You don't have to concern yourself with the matters of that family, dear. Now that we are married," he points to my ring, "it is no longer worth troubling over."

"I know, but I think they deserve an explanation at the very least, a reason for my involvement, and a promise that I will not be meddling in their affairs anymore. It will only take a moment, dear."

"Oh, all right. I suppose there is time for a small stop along the way, but you know we must make haste, or you will lose everything you own."

So this is truly goodbye to my career, my aspirations, and my only sense of identity. The two of us step out the door together without a second glance back.

# CHAPTER THIRTEEN

## 22 January 1901

The city whirls around me. The carts rattle as they pass me by, and the people speak in varied tones that all carry directly into my ears. The horses' hooves strike on the sidewalks meters away but the clops sound as if the horses trot right next to me. Every single sound bounces around my head, leaving me to sort through a myriad of noises. A coin clinks on the cobblestone, a cane tapping the sidewalk, a window opening, a bird chirping above, all swirl around my head. I can identify each one, yet it's foreign as it echoes through my head. As the sounds around me increase, my anger and frustration also begin to bubble under the surface. I stop dead in my tracks, trying to sort through the overwhelming abundance of details around me.

The rattle of the pebbles clattering underfoot on the cobblestone sings in my ears. It distracts from the assaulting, rotten stench of the city invading my nostrils. I drudge through all the fog that envelopes everything, mind and body. With each step, the music of the stones is drowned out and replaced with the screeching sounds of the other people walking. As the people pass, with each step, fragments of the conversations amongst the others loitering around grace my ears. The booming voices echo in my head, pulling me back to reality as civilians grumble at my impromptu decision to weave through all of the carriages, hand in hand with Teddy.

Under the sun's beams, the street appears radically different than it did the night before; it seems to be a new world. Every flaw is visible and cannot escape the scrutiny of the rays pushing down on them. Each hole in the road, shattered window, and piece of trash littering the streets illuminates the lifestyle of the people hiding under the night sky's cloak. However, there is still a façade put on by the people parading past in the daylight. As the horses trot by with women in their pristine petticoats and men in their impeccable suits, their hair is not out of place. The cruelty of the world has not touched these people, making them devoid of anything real or substantive. This picturesque image before my eyes is staged; this is not reality.

I keep my head down and continue walking, trying to avoid twisting my foot in the divots on the sidewalk. The busy clamor of the streets provides a different atmosphere than the one I had taken last night on my way to see the Yeats. It is not a change I relish in, for I prefer the walk that is rid of all the people dressed up in their masks.

"The queen is dead…"

"Long live the king…"

"What will England be like now?"

I arrive at the gothic cast iron gates, and a cold pang hits the palm of my hand as I push the door open. The intricate and ornate details engraved in the entrance are a menace to pass through, but once my foot crosses the threshold, I can turn my back to it and ignore the feeling of Death's hand in mine.

The mangled carcasses of the trees and their nearly barren branches bow to welcome the newest guests of the Yeats residence as if welcoming an old friend returning after a night away. Yet, there is no apple tree or roots poking up from under the grass. The mighty trunk of the tree we stood under just last night is gone and there is nothing to take its place.

"What happened to the tree from last night?" I ask Teddy.

"What tree?"

"The apple tree that was right here." I point to where the two of us quarreled last night.

"There was no tree here, darling. Are you alright?"

"Yes, there was! We both saw it!" I exclaim, resuming our skirmish from last night.

"Are you sure you're alright? There was nothing there last night, just as there's nothing here now!"

I sigh, and shake him away. I know what I saw last night, there's a reason Hudson let me stay with Scotland Yard for as long as I did.

Under the midday light, the house is quite different from how it appeared last night; no shadows are creeping around the property. Instead, it is hollow, and the emptiness echoes in my bones. The sunlight reflects off the shiny surfaces of the house, making the inside blinding and bleak to look at.

Teddy's footfall softens as he trails behind me, shying away from the face of the house, wanting to preclude any awkward questions about his presence here today. However, I am more focused on the Yeats family; they will never have an answer. They will forever wonder what happened to Cordelia, and will be forced to reconcile their grief with a feeling of incompleteness when they think of her. All of them deserve to know I tried my best.

"Do not overstay your welcome, dear," he warns.

"I am quite capable of judging that—"

"Are you sure? Your last interaction with them was… less than ideal." His face recoils at the reminder of the events that unfolded last night. "If you're not careful, they may follow through with their threat to call the constables."

Of course. He is right. A dull thud echoes through my ears as my fist hits the door once I have made my decision. *Thud. Thud. Thud.* The brass knob knocks slow and somber, matching each beat of dread from my old heart. What if they really do alert Scotland Yard? What if Hudson is not able to save me this time?

Perhaps this encounter would help liberate the secrets hanging between these beams and walls, suspended above those who wished to keep them out of sight, if not for my sake, then for theirs.

As my ears ring from the noise, a dreadful moment of panic again begins within my chest. Thoughts begin to race around my head at frightening speeds as I wonder if my decision is correct.

A sly voice in my head whispers the worst of what could happen. Perhaps this will only worry the Yeats more than necessary. Those secrets may vanish once they begin to fear judgment from others.

Fear can indeed cause people to do unpredictable things. Various delicate ecosystems can be destroyed in anticipation of the worst of what's to come; it is easier to set one's house ablaze oneself rather than waiting for the inevitable. Just as quickly as I made up my mind initially, I change it again. The Yeats need not know of my imminent end in this case until it is absolutely necessary.

A gust of wind slaps me as someone yanks the door inward, revealing a face haunted by grief.

"Mrs. Yeats, please forgive the intrusion—"

"Ah, Ms. Yoder. I see you've learned how to find the front door and knock," she says indifferently, her words stinging more than the slap of cold air. "You are not intruding… Not today, at least. What can I do for you?" Not a piece of her hazel hair is out of place, and her dress is more expensive than anything I have owned in the last several years, but her haggard face betrays her perfect appearance. Those who look in her eyes can see that she is fraying inside, barely able to contain her emotions.

Teddy is right. The Yeats hate me. Perhaps I should leave now before things get worse—

"Mother, get inside." A hand grabs Alexandra's wrist and yanks her into the darkness. "We answered all of your questions last evening and have nothing more to add. I think it's time for you to leave my family alone, mistress," he hisses, his words slithering from his tongue like a snake.

What is his problem? Has much changed since last night?

"Please." Pain explodes in my foot as Abraham tries to slam the door in my face but hits my toes instead. "I have only come to apologize, and my husband and I will be on our way. Please."

"Husband?" Alexandra inquires, gently nudging her son from the doorway. "Do not be ridiculous, Abraham." She turns back to me, and light spills on the porch as she opens the door wider. "My other two children have fallen ill with a chill and will not be joining us for dinner. We have two extra plates now. Perhaps you and your… husband would like to join us?"

"Mother," Abraham gasps, "she defiled Delia's room by—"

"Yes," she says, examining me from the doorway. "I can see it now. You're all grown up now, aren't you, Miss Yoder? You look just like your father." she breathes out.

"She still broke into—"

"Initially welcomed or not, she still managed to find more to help your sister than a team of constables in one evening. Abraham told me your name last night, and I remembered why you looked so familiar. I could not see you clearly in the night and the shock of your intrusion, but I can now. The gates will always open for you. You are a welcomed guest."

"Are you sure?"

"I am quite sure, Ann. Please join us."

"Teddy, it will only be a little while," I plead, wanting more than the measly crumbs cast aside by Hudson for dinner.

"Oh, all right, dear, but—"

"I know, I know. We must get home soon," I continue under my breath. I drag him through the entryway, passing the threshold from the outside world into the belly of the beast. We follow the current of the roll or red carpet to another set of mahogany double doors. The echoes of my heels tapping on the floor grow louder with each step—click, click, CLICK— crossing beneath the chandelier gently swaying with its beating flames and the staircase, dividing the body of the house into two separate chambers, inflated with different breadths of life.

The events of the day have exhausted me, and I find perhaps it would have been better for us to have gone home instead. A twinge of guilt stops my heart, and my lungs are solely responsible for my life as my mind races with thoughts of escape.

"Darling, I am only looking out for you." Sincerity oozes from his voice as he gently squeezes my hand.

Of course, he is right. He knows me better than anyone. After all, he is my husband now, I suppose.

A rumble from the weight of the heavy doors alerts everyone inside that it is open and that, at long last, it is time to eat. The table is already set with an array of dishes and cutlery lining the oblong table. Four plates are arranged one on all sides of the table, with a porcelain bowl of soup resting on top. A perfectly golden browned piglet rests on a silver platter as the centerpiece under the light of the lanterns mounted on the walls. Each pre-cut piece of meat is larger than the amount of ham I've eaten throughout my life.

"Dear." Alexandra's soft voice carries through the room as Abraham tries to sit at the head of the table. "We will leave those chairs for our guests. I am terribly sorry for my children's manners, or lack thereof. Please forgive them. These are trying times."

Before I can respond, Abraham replies, "I'm sure Mrs. Yoder has bigger concerns than where to sit!"

A whine escapes from the wooden chair as Abraham throws himself down, where his mother gestures for him to sit. The pattering of the carpet beneath the awkward shuffling of my feet echoes, despite the sound itself being so small.

Cutlery clinks inside the porcelain bowl as Alexandra takes the first bite, staring between Teddy and me, contemplating her next move, her next question.

"Once again, I must express how sorry I am for your loss," I begin.

"Ah, well, I would have still lost my child. Either way, even if she lived, I would never see her again…" Alexandra stares off into empty space as her eyes fill with tears. "But I suppose that is the life of a parent." She chuckles lightly, trying to lighten the mood. "We all slowly mourn a version of our children as we watch them grow into a new person… an adult." She glances up at Abraham, and he remains silent. Her love for her family is admirable, even if its suffocating nature ended up being her downfall.

"I was not aware you are married, Mrs. Yoder," she says, changing the topic. "How long have the two of you been together?"

My eyes dart emphatically to Teddy, unsure of what to say. Do I tell the truth? What if she gets upset? Do I lie? What if she sees right through that?

"We have only just been married, Mrs. Yeats," Teddy replies, deciding for me.

"Ah, well, congratulations are in order! I suppose now that you're not… erm… working, Mrs. Yoder. Is that still your surname?"

"Not anymore!" I exclaim. "As of today, I am now Mrs. Ambrose." The name is odd, and slides off my tongue in such a peculiar way.

"Well, Mrs. Ambrose, now the two of you should have time to cherish one another." The room livens as her smile of sincerity brightens each candle.

Cutlery clinks again, followed by a silence so loud that I wonder if I still possess the ability to hear. I stare up, looking across the room to see Teddy. Lanterns flicker as the walls shudder from the severe beating received on the front door, and this question is immediately laid to rest. The legs to Abraham's chair squeal as he rushes out of the room, marching out to see who is threatening his home.

"Mother!" he yells, and a thunderous footfall follows his voice. "Bring him here, right through these doors!" he shouts, guiding the strangers into a separate room.

In a swirl of her skirts, Alexandra whisks herself off, following the sound of her child's yells.

"Are you all right?" I hear from outside of the room. "Can you hear me?"

My hand jolts at the realization that someone is tugging on it, yanking the cutlery out of my hand as I can barely breathe and struggle to put two thoughts together.

"We should go, darling. We should not intrude on their time of need." The walls pass us in a haze of green as Teddy storms out, dragging me with him. Prying my hand free, I peek into the room next door, the source of the ruckus, before Teddy can say anything else.

"Baby, can you hear me?" Alexandra says soothingly.

"Yes," a voice rasps, barely audible among the commotion of the others in the room.

The blue uniforms pierce my eyes. I'd recognize those anywhere. A hoard of constables circles around the couch in the library, although I cannot see who they are fussing over.

"Darling," Teddy hisses, "we must leave now. This is, quite frankly, none—" I wave him away before he can continue.

"What happened? Why were you by the water? You know you can't swim!" her voice cracks.

"Are you stupid? You could've drowned, Albert!" Abraham shouts.

Every organ in my body is at risk of shutting off as my brain switches into overdrive trying to piece everything together. What's wrong? Why have the constables brought him here?

"I tried to stop her." No more information is given; his words and charisma are locked up.

"Stop her? From what? She is resting upstairs."

"No."

"Where is your sister?" his mother begs, unwavering in her sternness, but fear floods through the cracks of her words.

"She ran away."

"No," Alexandra gasps, unable to process the news.

"She took the ticket from Delia's room and decided to leave in her place."

"No, no, no, no, no." A reprisal of the melancholic melody sung for those on the hallowed grounds last night begins. With each word, Alexandra's wail grows unhinged, and the jaws of the monstrosity of grief residing in her heart open, unleashing its song of anguish once again.

"I tried, Mother. I tried to stop her," Albert cries, his sobs matching those of his mother. "But I was too late." He sniffles. "She was already gone. I made it to the docks, but she was no longer there. She left me to drown in the water."

"I'm sure she did not see you, or she would've—" Abraham begins.

"She left us," Albert says coldly.

"Shall we go after her, ma'am?" the constable interjects. "We can have people waiting for her when she lands. She will be brought back here on suspicion of murder—"

"Murder!" Albert exclaims.

"Yes, murder!" he howls. "It is quite odd that such an esteemed young lady would vanish without a trace, without a word so soon after—"

"She did not murder her baby sister, constable!" Alexandra shrieks, outraged at the idea.

"Darling, we need to go!" Teddy whines, pulling my arm, knocking me off my feet from the sudden change of balance.

"Do you have guests, Mrs. Yeats?"

"I have forgotten all about them!"

One constable peers through the crack in the door, locking into my gaze. Such a familiar set of eyes, one hazel and the other a clear blue.

Oh no.

"Hey, I know you!" he calls out.

No longer wanting him to disappear, I grab Teddy's arm and yank myself up from the ground. "I'm ready to go, now!"

Stumbling through the hallways, fumbling through the door, I wonder if we'll ever make it out in time.

"She's the escaped ghost who roams the halls of Scotland Yard at night!" he yells. "We must arrest her. Men!" I hear before launching from the house and into the crowd of people strolling through the city.

I wince as my ankle buckles from the sudden terrain change, from the grass to the cobblestone street. Horses yell at us as we run through the streets, not looking back to see our pursuers just behind us. We jump to the opposite side of the road and sprint through a dark, narrow alley leading to another part of the city. But to my dismay, the constables are still close behind.

"Where do we go?" Teddy asks.

"Well, if we keep running, I'm sure eventually they'll stop." I pant, barely able to finish my sentence without wheezing.

"No, I don't just mean at this moment. We need time to figure something out." Looking back, the blue coats are gone, and we are free to end this madness. Slowing our pace, we continue our conversation.

"I need to go get—"

"We do not have time! We must get out of this mess first."

"I can't leave what little I have! Not again!" I cry.

"Can't you see? The only way out is to leave now, while we are still one step ahead. We have to find a way to escape the city and get to my cousin's house. They will always be right behind us."

"I suppose you are right."

"Aren't I always?" He laughs between steps as we resume walking. "We can stay at his house for a short while until we can get our bearings in order with some peace and quiet."

"Are you sure we can't collect our things? It will only take a moment and we should still make it by night."

"There's no time," he chides, grabbing my arm, running past a group of constables congregating further up the street, trying to locate the two fugitives of the law, wanted dead or alive.

Why must we leave so fast? Surely we have time for a quick stop! I have no other choice but to follow Teddy. I gave up this decision when I signed my name away.

# Chapter Fourteen

## 22 January 1901

"Teddy, how far away is this cousin of yours?" I ask as the aggressive chop of the waves threatens to pull me under.

"Just a short journey, dear. We just have to row out to the small bit of land that should be right up here," he says, gesturing ahead.

"Where has he gone?" I ask, curious that a person would go through all this trouble to get to their house frequently. "Why is his estate empty now?"

"The tide is too rough for him to stay there during this time of the year," he replies, untying the fraying rope and keeping the dingy anchored to the slatted wooden docks. "He stayed and didn't leave for years but abandoned it long ago. He returns from time to time, but I doubt he would risk going again at a time like this."

"Are you sure we should risk this?" The waves grasp the last piece of my sanity, my calmness, with each tendril rising above the surface, and I fall into a sea of relentless questions. What if we drown? What if we cannot return? What if the boat capsizes and we are stranded? "I'm feeling a little uneasy about this. Perhaps we should find another place."

"We have no time! We have nowhere else to go!" he snaps. "We must hurry if we do not want to be guided to our death by the stars."

He is right. Besides, even if he isn't, there is nothing I could do to change what has already started. The storm resurges at this thought, raging on to do more damage to the few remaining structures standing within me. I have nothing else now, and perhaps that's for the best. With each word, a wave sweeps me away, dragging me beneath the surface and into the depths, drowning me.

I step into the boat as Teddy keeps it stable from the docks. Without a sound, he steps in, sinking the ship further down into the water with him, and we find ourselves staring at each other, just as we were a mere hour ago. I feel fuzzy as I think of the journey ahead as if my silhouette is no longer defined but blurry to anyone who lays eyes on me.

"I'm sorry for snapping at you like that." He takes my hand before continuing. "We just have so little time before we get carried out by the current, caught by the constables, or worse. We have no choice but to leave, and we only have now to do it."

Once again, he is right. "I should have listened, Teddy," I admit, defeated once again by his efforts to look out for me.

"Here," he grumbles, handing me an oar. "We will get there much faster if we paddle together."

The two of us row and keep rowing under the hazy curtain of gray clouds, darkening the bright sky behind. Each wave rocks the boat in a relentless movement so violent I wonder how a simple oar will keep us from tipping. We cut through the treacherous tides without a word, without a sound to save us from drowning in our own thoughts.

What do we do? What do we talk about? A thousand questions fill my head with the force of each wave pushing us further away from the mainland, further away from our connections, further away from socialization. Maybe we should turn back before it's too late to change our minds or get stranded.

A metal spire is the first sign of land to greet my eyes as if to ward off any unwanted signs of life from the grounds. This steeple is supported by a stone tower, allowing those inside the chance to look out to see the vast and desolate emptiness before them. Every face of the house has a transparent surface, reflecting each wave as a solemn reminder of their barren surroundings. The rest of the manor branches off from the tower, a large stone square that comes up to a sharp, angular point. There is no plant life anywhere surrounding the house, no garden, no trees, and not a single blade of grass pokes their heads from between the pieces of gravel leading up to the doorway.

"This is our final destination, dear." The boat rocks as he jumps out, tugging the hull with him as he wades in waist-deep water. Jagged stones scrape against the bottom of the vessel as Teddy pulls it to shore. He offers his hand out, and I take it, and he is my only support as I take one step followed by another. There is no more swaying, no more choppy waters, no more anything. "Let's go inside."

He holds his hand out for me to take.

"I want to go home," I say, keeping my arms firmly planted at my side. "I want to go back."

"We are home, darling!"

"You know what I mean. I want to go back to my home in London."

"What home?" he yells. "There is nowhere for you to return to! This is your home!"

"We can find something," I ask, desperate to get back in the boat. "The Yeats, or Hudson—"

"We've been over this over and over again! We cannot do that!" Each word is more aggressive than the last. "You are homesick for a place that never existed, one that never will exist."

"Why are you so eager to keep me here?" I shout above the water rising in my chest. "You've been relentless in your efforts to drag me here! I offer solutions, and you don't accept them! I suggested this same idea months ago, and you refuse to entertain it! Why are we here now?"

"We weren't ready for this then! We weren't married then. Now we are!" he teases, holding out his hand once again. "And I have a wedding gift for us, Annie!"

Hand in hand, we continue up the beaten path, stumbling over the ground, but these pebbles are the least of our problems.

"Teddy, the boat!" I yell, remembering our only way off the island. "The current will take it away!"

Tripping over the rocks, blundering over the uneven terrain, we make it to the shore in time to see the ocean pick up the ship, carrying it out of reach, disappearing beneath the waves. Our way home is gone forever.

What have I done? What have I done?! I'm stuck here now, with no one to save me. Nowhere to go. How do I leave? I cannot swim, and without a boat there is no escape.

"Darling, it's all right! We can figure something out, but I need to tell you something else now!"

I take a breath, trying to recompose myself, but am unsuccessful in this attempt. If I can find a room to sit with my thoughts, I can find a solution. I'm sure of it.

"We should go inside," I say, carefully articulating each word under the slurred speech of my drunken stress.

He stretches out his hand, and I take it as the two of us walk up to the door, steady, somber, and silent.

He pulls my arm back as we reach the front door.

"Darling." He turns to me with a goofy grin. "We have to do this properly. Let me carry you through the door."

"You are aware that this tradition is only for people who own the house, right?"

He breathes out, bringing his hand up to his neck. "Actually, that is what I wanted to show you." Light radiates from his smile. "This house is ours now. It's our home now."

"H-how?!" is the only word I can get out.

"I wrote to my cousin. He told me he moved ages ago. The house has sat here, empty since then, and now it belongs to us."

"I-I don't understand." The air does not fill my lungs, no matter how many breaths I take. "If this was an option, why didn't you tell me? Why did you lie?"

"Oh." He looks down. "You're upset!"

"You lied to me!"

"But it's better this way! The two of us can stay together forever now. There will be no more files, no more machines, nothing but the two of us."

"We didn't have to get married! We still could've done that without a contract! There is no way out for me!"

"We agreed on the other reasons! It was only a matter of time!"

"The tide is coming in, we need to go inside, or we'll have no choice but to join our boat at sea," is all I can say. Can anything else be said to justify what has happened?

The wind howls as Alexandra did as she held her dead child in her arms, cursing those who pried her baby from her too soon.

What will become of the Yeats now? What will Alexandra choose to do with her own rotten apples? Cordelia will rest without peace now. If I stayed, perhaps—

*Thud.* Teddy slams the door behind me, trapping the two of us inside.

Ocean water rattles the windows in their frames as it crashes against the panes. The house shudders at the lash, retreating in hopes of avoiding such hostile treatment again. Yet the water inches closer and closer to the sides of the house, threatening to drown us all and keep our bloated bodies without leaving a witness to bear its crime.

"Do you remember," he says, placing his other hand on my waist, "the last time we danced like this?"

One step forward, two steps back.

"Feels like a lifetime ago." I chuckle as the walls tremor from another fearsome wave.

One step forward. We pass the outline of rooms lining the hallways of the sides of the house, but there is nothing in any block. Two steps back. No people, no furniture, no lanterns. Striped green wallpaper absorbs any light reflecting through the windows, washing out the stone slabs on the ground, absorbing any inkling of warmth. A thin line of frayed carpet trails the baseboards. We follow the red veins down the hallways and through the house.

The walls expand and contract with each movement as a pair of lungs breathes when running from a formidable foe. One step forward, two steps back.

"Just think, we have nothing but time to worry about here. The stresses of work and the city are far away," he says.

"I know how long you've dreamed of leaving that factory." *Crash*. The wave speaks over me. "It is quite the miracle that you've lasted as long as you have, unscathed from the machines after all these years." *Crash*. One step forward. "How did you manage that?" Two steps back. *Crash*.

"Nothing more than being careful and mindful of my actions."

"Teddy." *Crash*. One step forward. "How have you remained so well fed with such low wages?" *Crash*. Two steps back.

The house struggles to breathe beneath the waves, fighting to stay above the water and remain intact.

"I had a great provider." He grins. "After the night we met when you asked me to come into our house."

But that's not how the story went! He was not invited, he simply appeared at my house! One step forward, two steps back as mud squelches underfoot amidst the dance.

"Teddy!" The flickering flames fade as I stop in the middle of the hallway. "Quit trailing mud into the house! Where does it all come from?!"

Silence

"Look at all of this! The carpets are stained. It'll be impossible to get it all out!"

"It's just cloth!" he cries back. "It's barely still red and hanging on the floor by a thread! A little mud will be fine!"

"No, it is not!" The carpet bunches up as he drags his feet under the force of my grip on his wrist. "It goes all the way down this hallway and up to each door! We haven't been here this long, and I'm sure the rooms are already dirty! Will this room be dirty too?"

A squeal stabs my ear as I shove the nearest door in.

"No!" he shouts, scrambling to grab the handle and close the door once more, but he is too late.

Light from the lanterns behind me bleeds into the room, revealing a suitcase sitting on a bed in front of me. Gold lettering shimmers on the top of it, and I do not need to take a step further to know that the initials are my own. The letters AY beckon me home.

# Chapter Fifteen

## 22 January 1901

"What is my suitcase doing here?" My voice is shrill from shock.

"You don't remember?" He chuckles lightly. "You packed it just in case you needed to leave with no warning."

"No, that was years ago. That was before the fire," I breathe. "I lost it in the flames. I lost everything! How is this here?!"

"As I said, this is our home now. It would not be complete without a token of yourself."

It's not possible. This shouldn't be possible.

"We can restore this house how it once was. We can make it look like our old home. The bones are the same."

"How is my suitcase here?" I roar, sending another tremor through the walls. "Why am I here?"

"Because we are home, dear. Must we go through this again?" he huffs, swaying the house.

"You pressured me to leave the Yeats' house at dinner." My finger digs into his shoulder as I jab it toward him. "You pushed me to leave everything. You brought me here. Why?"

"For your safety! For our safety!"

"No! Do not lie to me again." The waves threaten to drown my words. "You have been involved in the Yeats case since the beginning."

"What an outlandish accusation! You asked for my help!"

"No! Never once did I ask for help with the Yeats. You invited yourself. Why?"

"Are you asking what I think you are?"

"Why?" The question rises above the boom of thunder rolling in with the frightening clouds.

"The constables already said Adelaide is responsible for this heinous crime! Are you happy? I do not need to justify myself like this to you!"

"Yes." The admission of guilt rings through my head, shouting over my whisper. "I am. Why did you kill her?"

"I just told you." He flails his hands around in anger.

"How do you know her sister's name?"

"The constables said—"

"Why did you murder her?" I roar. "Her name was never mentioned by them or by me. I am not stupid, Teddy."

A cool, collected laugh rings through the room, without any furniture to block the echoes from reaching me. "She would've never survived in this world."

Is this how I die? If I do not become his next victim, will I survive trapped beneath the rubble of this broken house as it topples from the storm bashing against its body?

"Because of you, we'll never know!" I scream. "She was just a child."

"You were just a child too," he mutters. "There may be blood on the floor, but my hands are clean."

"What is that supposed to mean?" The windows shake as a breath trapped in a pair of lungs rattles. "You came into my house all those years ago, and this is what you do! I'd like you to go."

"Please don't make me go."

"Go! Leave my house."

"I was trying to be polite, dear. But this home is mine, legally and by blood. If anyone is leaving, it will be you."

"But how can I?" I point to the waves pushing against the windows and doors, blocking all exits. "There is no boat, thanks to you! Get out! Get out! Get out!"

His laugh resumes, trapping me as a spider's silk traps unsuspecting prey. "I will not make this easy for you, Annie," he hisses, and each word slithers closer to me. "You foolish child," he continues, seeing the vacant expression in my eyes. "Blood of my blood, we are the same, you and I."

No. This is not possible. No. We are different; we have had two separate lives.

"I am part of you, and you are a part of me." Words rattle like chains keeping me tethered to him.

"Who are you?"

"I am the darkness lurking around every street corner." With every word, he takes one step closer. "I am the Anxiety that plagues every mortal. I am the virus that lives on the brain. The illness that ravages the heart. The parasite that digests your organs with each breath. I am the mind folding in on itself, ripping holes in the lives of unsuspecting people." His stone-cold eyes stare directly through me, no longer seeing me as a person. "Are you truly unaware? Truly as ignorant as all of the others?" I jump out of my skin at his uproarious laughter. "Humanity needs me. You need me. Without me, you'd be quite useless." The venom spewing from his mouth spreads, shaking its branches in my mind.

A liquor seeps from the hems of his tightly fitting pants and from the sleeves of his jacket, resting snugly around his wrists until Teddy no longer stands in front of me. A creature morphing into various shapes replaces him. A young boy emerges from the debris of the sludge, the same young boy who knocked on my door when I was a child.

"You killed a little girl!"

"Do not interrupt me, Annie! She brought her fate on herself," he continues. "It's impossible to be convicted of a murder that never happened."

"That's not possible! I saw her! I saw her family!"

"Who's to say what happened outside of these doors? What is reality to one, is nothing more than a nightmare to another. People can try to abandon their homes, only to end up right where you stand, but you should know better than anyone. How many homes have we abandoned over the years, Annie? You all end up back in the same place no matter how many faces are given to your problems. You can stay, plot, and run away from these problems but someone is always stuck cleaning up the pieces. Yes, a child died, but whose was it?"

"But… but she's just a girl. You're just a child now. How is this possible?" Flashes of the horrors I had witnessed the previous night danced under my eyelids and refused to leave. The wails whisper in my ear and replaying for an absent audience. The haunting image of the gaunt faces of the family will forever be worn as a brand on my mind.

"I do not discriminate." His whisper guts me. "I take the form of what's needed to survive, as a chameleon changes colors or as a cheetah blends into the savannah."

Liquor continues pouring on the stone floors, oozing from his body as smooth as he once spoke, drawing me near into his kiss of Death. His eyes turn into beady black dots, and his mouth morphs into a grotesque grin that curls up at the corners. The changes continue until I stare at a face I no longer know—an elusive figure who knows no physical bounds or limitations in its insatiable desire to consume anything in its path.

"But why?" I beg. "Why?"

"There's not always a motive, Annie." He laughs coolly. "A source of life, a host, in exchange for my survival. I saw a window of opportunity. There was a new victim, a new life on the other side of the door, the night I knocked; I was eager to feast off it again."

"Wasn't she enough? What more do you need? What more is left to take?" I shriek. Wails and screams build up in my chest; the pressure is so great it feels as if I will burst. "I want to go back to my home! Take me back to Scotland Yard! I don't care where you take me but get me off this godforsaken island!"

"Darling," he says slowly. "We've already discussed this. That is impossible! Besides, why would you want to leave the place you've spent your whole life? Much like your homes, you've created her in your own delusions." His voice echoes through the barren house. "You only see a child from the memories you wish to remember and all that's left is a monster pieced together from the bits you wish to forget."

"No, you did this to me! Look at where I am, and look at what you've taken from me!"

"Don't be ridiculous!" He laughs.

*Leave me alone. Just leave. Please leave me alone.* My whole body becomes an empty void of nothingness and numbness, wanting nothing more than to sleep away this exhaustion. But I suspect sleep would not fulfill this ache, for this is tiredness not of the body but of the soul.

"As you wish, dear." His coy smile sends a chill down my spine. How could he hear me without words?

He morphs into an oozing puddle, absorbing into the floorboards and creeping up the walls. The goo sinks into the wallpapers, and the scratched emerald paper that stared at me earlier pierces me with its damask eyes.

The beams groan as they hold the burden of Teddy once again, desperate to cleanse these cursed corridors of him.

Do I lay here, trapped in the web of this Anxiety smeared along the walls? Do I throw myself in the water to rid my lungs of this stale air? Do I spend my life roaming the halls as a ghost once again, brain-dead?

Rattling chains echo through the hallways, the mournful song of regret bellows through the bones of the building, as the chirp of a caged bird cries for the freedom of its un-ensnared days. Wails ricochet through the rooms, hoping they will be greeted by the friendly face of Mercy but are forced to reconcile with the grievous face of the tortured soul who uttered these horrid shrieks.

The cold stone slabs under my knees are unyielding in their reminders of my banishment to this island. There is nowhere to go, nowhere to flee to without risking drowning in the unrelenting tide of the sea around me.

How could I have been so foolish? How did I not see this? Thoughts ram into the side of my head, and I cannot conjure any other ideas or memories than those forever seared in my brain. You should've seen this. You should've seen the signs. Stupidity and ignorance are the only excuses. How ironic it is to be the detective examining the murder of your own mind.

I am nothing more than what became of the poor little girl. Although my body is not decomposing, my spirit is as good as dead. My aspirations have broken down into the soil, my heart has withered away in the wind, and the brittle bones of my existence remain waterlogged under the rising tide of my tears. Will I stay this way forever, detached from my body, living in limbo with nothing but my unyielding thoughts for company? Unable to look at my life except through the window?

The clock chimes two-twenty-two once more, as it shall be tomorrow and every day after. And so here I'll remain, damned to rummage through my mind, what's left of it at least. Doomed to be a prisoner given a life sentence for a crime that never happened. Alone at sea, unable to leave this desolate prison without drowning in the tide, and without a hand to pull me up. Here my body lies while my mind rots. And all I can think of is the cursed child, cursed to live her days resting in a wooden box under the suffocating weight of the world.

And so I remain alive, with nothing but the bloated organs of a decaying carcass to keep me breathing. The frantic fantasies of escape have left, carried out by the tide, never to return once they realized they could not pull me under the water. They have been replaced by the relentless wave of "what ifs", with no one else to help free me from these notions. I am doomed to spend eternity here, mulling over every prospect, every memory, over and over until my body breaks apart as my mind has. Nothing could have been done to save the poor child, but there was for me. I am forced to relive my regrets and experiences until I have exhausted every story and clue I can use to blame myself for my imprisonment. I am a merciless judge and require every shred of evidence to satisfy my predetermined verdict.

# CHAPTER SIXTEEN

## 21 February 1901

Days come and go, and the sun is ruthless in its reminder of the time slipping from my grasp. Teddy has made his presence unknown since that fateful night, but the wallpaper droops from the walls from his weight. Although a fleck of mud will appear on the carpet, I will know where he waltzed the corridors once again. Some days, a rock will wait for me outside my bedroom door, and I'll see that he roamed the garden while thinking of me. I suspect it is only a matter of time before he returns to strike a conversation or resume our dinners in the dining room.

The front door remains firmly shut. I sit on the threadbare carpet anchored on the stairs, and the water recedes between the floor and the door. The ground dries, causing all proof of the storm to vanish, and I am left to piece my house and mind back together.

How am I supposed to fix this? If I stay here and wait, will Father walk through the door again? Just as he did eight years ago? Will he fix the splintered banister and rotten floorboards as if nothing ever happened? No. The only person who will step through the door again is me. And Teddy, I suppose, much to my dismay. The mornings spent cutting him from the house with glass shards are in vain.

"Go away! Leave me alone!" I scream, ripping the wallpaper from the wall, but the damask stays the same. Tearing these pieces of parchment accomplishes nothing more than doing more damage to the few salvageable structures in the house.

While I stay here, stewing in the same stale air, I am at risk of being next. Is he resting to claim another victim? Has he already claimed one?

From now until the end of this house's lifetime, there shall be proof to testify to the parasite that ravaged these halls and still looms in the shadows. It will be impossible to scrub the mud out of the carpet after years of infection, especially with only the efforts of one day of cleaning behind me. The red cloth is nailed to the floor; it cannot be ripped out. Splintered wood, broken pencils, dirty rocks, and shattered lanterns can be thrown back into the ocean, never to be seen by another person. I can smooth over the tears in the remaining scraps of wallpaper, but the scars and barrenness will always echo the mother's song at the loss of her child.

The tide recedes further with every passing day. Glass shards clutch their place in the panes, refusing to budge from their homes. I suspect with a bit of paint, these cracks have the potential to outshine all other stained glass tapestries simply because it is the one that belongs to me and tells the story of my survival last night.

This house will never be restored to its original glory, but it can be habitable if I put in the work. The library will never be as grand as the one I had growing up, but my own stories and memory will have to suffice. The kitchen will remain devoid of any real sustenance, but nothing can be done. There are nothing but hollow bones of the fish that once roasted above the hearth and a single rotten apple sitting on the shelf. I have yet to decide what to do with it. Do I discard it with the other rubbish? Or keep it?

*Thud.* Has he come back? I race down the hallway to see my suitcase falling on its side as it stands next to the pile of broken pieces of the house by the front door. Is today the day I rid my home of this clutter? Who knows how long the tide will remain tame like this?

Am I foolish to believe that if I stand by the shore, the boat will wash on the banks again? Perhaps. But should I ever decide to leave, this is my only hope. Although, what is the point of ever leaving here? After all, this is my only home and the only one I'll have for the rest of my days. I cannot and will not remarry if I wish to not end up as those other women living on the streets. Besides, as long as Teddy lives and our marriage remains legally binding in contract, it will not be possible. We are the same in the eyes of the law, for better or worse.

I cannot give this house up. The inside needs to be fixed, and the ghosts of the past will still haunt it till the end of time. But it's my only home and the only one I'll own in this lifetime. It is mine and mine alone, despite what any law would like to say.

Besides, if Teddy's existence remains confined to these walls, I see no reason to abandon this house. There are no other options to pursue. I suppose I should not complain. I have a roof over my head, protection from the storms, and new grounds to walk through. This is more than before. An improvement is still an improvement. And I have to admit that the shore can be nice to ponder on from time to time. Although the same fish dinner night after night is enough to make anyone sick of thinking about it just once more.

Bone and glass stab my palms with each trip from the door to the beach. Why wait any longer to get rid of these remnants? Today is as good a day as any to pick up the pieces from the destruction from the breakage last night.

Wind combs through my hair as I lift my dress to wade in the water, far away from the final resting place of the pieces of the house I threw in moments ago. A scrap of wallpaper rustles in the breeze, fluttering between my fingers like an animal wriggling in my hand for freedom. "There is no way to say this to you directly," I look up from the words I wrote on the paper and stare at the water, "so I have to hope the waves will relay this message to you." My voice catches, and I want to yank them from my throat without having to make a sound. "To the mother without her child, I am sorry that you have no choice but to carry this burden to your grave. To the child who died, I am sorry you weren't protected. And, to the child who never lived, I am sorry you never got to taste the rich experiences of the world. Little one,

I am sorry that the murder of your youth was for naught."

The wind takes the paper from my hand as I let go. My lungs rattle as I take another breath, and I continue saying the words that have remained unsaid until now.

"We lived as children, but now you no longer breathe. Our childhood was murdered by the same creature, and in that, we are the same. A silly suitcase would've never solved our problems." I chuckle at this commonality between us. "But we had to learn the hard way, I suppose. We can be mad at this loss, and believe me, I am mourning for the both of us, but what's done is done. There is no point in drowning in the ocean of grief as we try to swim after what has been taken, what was never truly ours to control. We cannot swim in something so vast and expect to stay afloat. That's not how life goes."

My knees groan as I crouch to sit on the sand and jagged rock chunks. Water dances between my fingers as I stroke the waves. "I guess we weren't given many options but to leave if we wanted to live," I continue. "But I keep finding myself in the same place. Back at my house, packing my suitcase and waiting, just as you did, I'm sure. I keep coming and going to those memories as I please, to return to that moment, to visit this grief, wondering why we had to give it up sooner than most. What we wouldn't do for just one more minute in our homes before everything happened. What would our lives be like today? Maybe I would work with my father, and perhaps you would still be alive." I breathe out as that thought washes me away. "I blamed myself for not sending him away sooner, but I see now that it is not my burden to bear. Just as your murder is not yours either. There was no one else but you, me, and who we had to become along the way. We were doomed from the beginning." A sob escapes, and I wipe a single tear away, returning it to the ocean.

"We can cry and grieve and open our doors to familiar faces, but the pain will always linger, and the house will always be dimmer than before. Here." I pull the suitcase on my lap and push it into the tides. The current graciously accepts the gift and carries it on its back, promising to return it to the place it belongs. "Take this. Nothing inside is for me anymore. Everything in it was made for you. The dresses no longer fit because I've grown while you can't. I can't hold onto it anymore. I want you to have it, but know that you don't have to take it. You can let go of yours too and watch it sail into the horizon, as I am doing now. It no longer belongs to me, and it never should've been waiting for me, for us, to use it as we did."

Water washes over my feet one last time, and I stand up, straightening my skirts. "I shall remember you forever. I regret that we had to meet in such circumstances, but now I know you can rest easy. I am so sorry, little one."

And just like that, the knife is pulled from my heart, and the needle in my hand patches the hole in the heart up. Maybe now the whole of the heart will beat again without the cold knife blade there to remind it of its mortality.

Step by step, I trudge up to the door, taking my place again as acting lady of the house, passing the rocks asking to be found, the clouds plotting their next storm, and the fresh heap of soil anxiously waiting for a tree to sprout from the seeds of a rotten apple core.